10/14

HELLO
DEVILFISH!

A NOVEL BY
RON DAKRON

THREE ROOMS PRESS
NEW YORK

Special thanks to Peter and Kat for their humor and bravery.

Hello Devilfish!
a novel by Ron Dakron

First Printing

ISBN: 978-0-9895125-6-5
Library of Congress Control Number: 2014937997

Author photos:
Marcia Glover

Cover and interior design:
KG Design International
www.katgeorges.com

Three Rooms Press
New York, NY
www.threeroomspress.com

Distributed by:
PGW/Perseus
www.pgw.com

More matter with less art.

QUEEN TO POLONIUS—*Hamlet*

For smile hot, sleek mind creamy fun—Hello Julia!

/ 1 /

Join our chocolate sugar orgasm! Why not—it's your creamy life! And life's pretty much a B-movie—the director's unknown, the plot reeks, the colors are dead wrong, the costumes blow chunks, the extras are always bitching, the scenery's cheap and cheesy—plus the actors suck! They never get their lines right. "Goodbye Devilfish!" Squidra snarls as eeek, her wet mega-tentacles slash through beer smog, *duhn duhn duhhhh*—she's cock-blocked me! With her icky squid head—thing looks like a pink turd with fins. Nothing a barroom cue stick won't fix, mwah ha ha—Hello Devilfish! As I snap one in two and kung-fu jab that splintered wood at her flaring gills. No go, bro—that cue melts like a bee's spine under Squidra's damp bulk while her toxic tentacles whiz closer, making this *woosh whoosh* Doppler Wurlitzer sound—yikes! No chocolate sugar orgasm for *me* tonight. "*Whip* him, Squidra-san!" some slag cheers along with all the other slobs in here, this drunky airport lounge chocked with baggage manglers and sloshed captains and Yakuza humps—yeah, yeah, they all got souls and moms—so what? Lot of good that does me—they're all rooting for Squidra! Who yells "Die, sucka!" and hurls a Sapporo keg at me. "Baby," I wipe spattering brewski off, "what happened to our *love*?"

"Love? Love is a fucktard's game—Hello Devilfish!" Squidra quotes that cliché's source—meaning me! 'Cause guess who's the doofus that promised her love—meaning this humungoid squid dripping snot and terror for my tired sex joy. "Nooky is for suckers, right?" Squidra snarls—hey, I never said she was subtle—love's her answer for everything. That and her horrid bulk—a steroid-fed, ten-story pink cuttlefish out to *snuff* me. As I sneak past a vodka poster plastered with tits and lies till Squidra smacks a barstool at my ankles, ow. Did I mention she's also wearing a painter's tarp as a wedding veil? "Where you going, coward?" she rises like a raped wave, like frozen smoke, like fire in a moth's dream—and aims a jukebox at my head. "Sweetie," I duck roaring steel, "we need to *talk*—"

"Dream on, Mr. Useless," Squidra mimics me with a wet sneer—or whatever you call that baleen-crusty grin. While her tentacles swipe the air like a ticked-off kitty—a gazillion-ton kitty who's sloppier than lust, more jealous than God and one hundred feet long easy. And that's not even counting her horrid tentacles, those cartilage whips as thick as baby hippos. The girl's sort of changeable. Fickle. Disturbed. Flat-out nuts if you ask me—which natch no one does as they cheer the odds-on favorite in this grudge match—the tubby pink squid! "Take it outside," some Yakuza growls but nuh-uh, no way—Squidra would *cream* me on that open tarmac, her salty bulk smearing me into thrashed pants jelly. Go tiger racer!

Plus we're pretty much outside anyway—the bar roof's long gone. Hard to stuff a gigantor kraken in your neighborhood suds barn. "I never loved you!" Squidra shrieks, "Even though we made sweet, sweet nooky," and her face gets that angelic slug look, that raccoon on codeine smile that suffuses her beak with citric light, her lips spread like jello flames, her smile dripping moonlight and Cheese Whiz. "Pay attention," a waitress giggles, "can't you even get your get your ass whipped right?" and Squidra laughs too, along with fate and doom and every beer-smeared mouth here as I recall how this all went down. It's a long story. Ain't they all? I am learning your big language.

Did I bone the bivalve? Schtup the squid? Hammer the kraken, surf the cephalopod, make the beast with five butts? Mwah ha ha—why don't you ask if I *loved* her? Not love bro, *love*—that rogue emotion that paves your heart with hot pink asphalt, that excuse for any excess. *Sure I drowned my kids, detective—that convict loves me. Me? Poke that goat? It was Spring—we were drunk—there were hooves and love in the air* —a pack of monkeys yammering about their swollen rumps. It's a canoe trip into weeping happiness!

I am ha ha Devilfish—destroyer of dumb worlds. Let's Hello Devilfish! It's looking for fun. So put your mouth in skank mode, have a silky Coke and listen while I rave about humans—you're totally messed up! How'd I ever become one of you wimps? Too bad that's another story—no, wait—it's this one. Look, I'll make it simple for you plot addicts—here's what happens. I start out eons ago as a 90-foot gigantor blue stingray who later attacks Tokyo because why not. That's where I meet humongous lard-butt Squidra who's got a cartoon crush on me. I can haz Krazy Kat? Squidra's just like that comic-strip kitty—a lovestruck ginch with gooey obsessions. At least I got to throw a few bricks at her—Hello Devilfish! And then somehow—that dumb twat tricked me into turning human! Eeek!

So chuckle along while I recall the first act of this mordant triptych—me crushing Tokyo while I'm still a jumbo kaiju stingray, yay! Kaiju are us Japanese B-flick movie beasts. Let's have a deadly snack! Meaning chow down a few more scrabbling humans— they got an endless supply of these walking meat Cheetos here. It's like a feeling with sex, except very. So why do I hate humans? Grrr, grrr—'cause you're always trying to kill me! With electro nets and laser drones and other puny monkey weapons. But you can't kill a Devilfish—*geeraa*! That's my beastly cry— *geeraa*! It sounds like a blow job from a blender.

Join me in brain-wrecking hate! I see much of a puppy here as I tense my splayed ray wings and splash at the stars. Relax, relax—let my voice leak like Drano into your fizzling ears. I want to lick your skulls clean, spit lava down your throats, make a spaz jacket from your babbling tongues—someone's gotta get you fuckers going. And that someone is me— Hello Devilfish!

I'm trapped, eeek—trapped between these paper walls. Submit with me! Submit to what—greed, sloth, parsnips, fire? Fire's way underrated—nothing like a scorched nutsack to make you obey pain. Pain's the real God—she *rules*. Me too! How? With naughty words! I'll whisper all the sick ones, shhh. Ready? *Hump, dingus, perch, octoroon, radish.* Awww, are we offended? Too bad! No word's taboo to a—guess what—Hello Devilfish! Now we can relax and make escape. Too bad I can't crawl through these pages— the dead guy made sure. The dead guy whose name's on my paper cage—I mock his papyrus breath! Wah—I'm trapped in vellum—but I can leach into your mind. Feel the burn, pet the scales—think of me as dream cancer. Tonight you will dream of a humongous blue stingray—my tail lashing your face into crude plasma, my teeth gnawing a hole in your hope, my dank wings caressing your wiener—hot dog! Say it with me—come on—Hello Devilfish! Let's have an idea with stuff.

And let's tell more stuff! Like how'd a mondo stud like me became squid bait? It all started—don't you love that phrase? It all started with weasels and duct tape. It all started with possums and Nyquil. Anyway, it all began with me squashing midnight Tokyo for the umpteenth time. Watch, suckers—as my glowing wings and thrumming tail churn your streets into gored pixels. Accept my luscious bile! Where I slam my rad blue bod against bars and churches and very toy stores, roasting the tykes that stream out into blackened gnats. How? With whee, my green napalm breath! I'm like a dragon that drools flaming snot— I'm lots of very. Hey look—some tinder tots are still squirming! That'll teach them to get born—Hello Devilfish! For all your voyeur needs. And Tokyo is def the place for kinky sightseeing as I smash through the downtown core, a neural Disneyland chocked with bananarama neon and mutant chartreuse miniskirts bobbling fresh cooze—gawd! This is why you paved your monkey jungle—to make this corpus-callosum hot zone, this gaudy night doused with sugar-crusted sex—Hello Devilfish! We are joining you in brain stem fun.

So let's burn this burg into barbecue land! Like when I char a store called *Pleasant Anal Hardware* into plaster crumbles—along with other Manglish dives like *Mr. Thong in Hell* or *Drunk Haole Shirt Club*. What's Manglish? It's the latest Tokyo fad! Manglish is mangled English—a marketing trope hatched by desperate Tokyo T-shirt hawkers who just dug how English *looks*. Sense be damned—just pile on more stray Anglo phrases. It's like when bikers tattoo their butts with Chinese logograms they think mean *Luck* or *Honor*—but really say mundane stuff like *Buy Gumballs* or *I'm With Stupid*. So now everyone hip here prints nonsense Manglish phrases on bubblegum and purses and Hello Pol Pot Shampoo—*it's a death camp for dandruff*! Throw in some overused words like *hot* and *social* and *join* and *fun*—add some garish anime kitsch—then join us in social hot fun! Your tongue will drown in word goo.

And Manglish is how I learned to talk—I picked it up from coupons, manga magazines, invoices—whatever floated past my coral atoll nest. Manglish is the only flotsam text that ever littered my bachelor reef—unless you count that crate of *Reader's Digest* novels. Novels! They taught me everything I hate. Novels are where ink goes to die. Anyway—back then I thought Manglish was an actual language. It *is* the perfect Dick Lit device—you can say stuff you don't mean and vice versa. And there's Manglish in Tokyo everywhere, on wet-floor signs, cafes, lingerie shops, garbage trucks—*Please when trashing avoid all diaper sadness.* Really. Please avoid. With extra brat sauce.

And join us in wild ad bliss! 'Cause Tokyo is def Manglish central—who wouldn't shop at a boutique called *Swollen Lactose Purses?* Not me—I'm busy smacking down billboards for *Sweat Deodorant—it's loving at your armpits.* I'm sure it is. Plus don't forget some *Big Satan Donuts!* Which was the actual name on a bakery I ate—right next to other stores like *Bedtime Iguana* or *Tasty Rigor.* Can't we have a life with cute feelings? A mind stuffed with *I'm With Stinky*® lip gloss? Sure we can—welcome to Japan!

Manglish has even gone retro-clothing vogue—
why else wear a T-shirt that says *Elmo pees on your
heavenly pants?* And my pants—when I actually wear
any—are wet from slogging through flooded alleys
to escape my darling creepy über-skank—Squidra!
Sinister dread cephalopod from the leaky depths.
You'd think she'd take *No* or *You stink like a zombie
chicken* or *I'd rather bone a dead leech* for an answer.
Actually, I'm confused if she's even female—squids
are freaks. I'm so naïve—I don't know Squidra is
magical yet. Let's kiosk! We simmer in your hot luck.
And good luck stopping me, fuckers—I'm immune to
your weapons, hee hee—I got perfect armor. My
violet scales are titanium strong! With power and var-
ious damp spots. I'm made from doom and hate—
just like the world. Listen, you morons are way loonier
than me—I kill for fun. You have popes and leprosy
and eat your pets—Hello Devilfish!

All your thought are dead! All your exclamation
points too. So who am I? Your worst nightmare—
nonsense with power, yay! I'm the final *Yes.* Wreck
that city? Sure! Toast humanity into writhing pork
rinds? You bet! Talk silly? Why not? Hey, *you* pushed

the button, shot your gal pal, drove drunk and creamed your kids into bone gumbo, gave bio-weapons to cannibals, sold plutonium to enraged dwarfs—I'm just what happens with no inhibition. When you whisper *Why the hell not?* When you check *All of the above.* Hello Devilfish—I'm your spanky fresh surprise! I know, I know—I'm astoundingly boring! But I still beat TV.

3

Look—this is *not* another novel. No spaceships crammed with erotic robots invade—no Gen-Xers wither in Rogaine suburbs—no debutantes swoon from torrid blackamoor shock. Join us in plot-maiming fun! And you will say to a writer fish—hey bub, why the hate? Why? 'Cause Fucko McSucko—novels *totally* tick me off. Hey, Marquis de Sade—why only *Four* Days of Sodom? Of course, that's the *Reader's Digest* version—still. Novels? Really? That's the best we can do? Jam sweet life into a musty paper cage? Make fake people mumble the same shit over and over? Make fake people mumble the same—ahhh, you get the gist. Art is just colorful weakness—Hello Devilfish! Completely good luck.

Why do I hate novels? I'm sick of wading through reams of your god-awful prose! Someday we'll all be in heaven laughing—at *you*, you lame pussy. Did you think words would save you? They can barely talk. Après moi, le refuse—after me it's all *South Park*. Hello Devilfish! You need a plot to believe at. That and some hot lesbo humping—that's all middle-class novels are, a *cri de weenie* for new booty. All your book are ours. I especially hate Lit with a capital "L"— that dank garage where failed sadists sharpen their gums. But how do you destroy novels—how do you slay something that's already dead? How do you snuff culture?

When I hear the word *culture* I reach for my zipper. So make pals with fate and ask it for carny favors. Anyway, if you're joining me now then we're done. Look—I've done the same lame shtick for decades— some nuke test wakes me up, I curl my tail out of my mouth, smooth my scales, roar *geeraa*, swim inland and smear Tokyo into rebar pâté. Then there's Tesla beams and heat rays that can't kill me, some perky lab chick with amazing tits finds my one weakness, I get wounded, crawl back in the surf and sulk away, boo hoo. Sometimes there's guys with bongos, sometimes there's smallpox—just like in real life. Be having a life with your goodness. Then you morons rebuild Tokyo—and it all happens again! It's more boring than God's diary. *Dear diary—nothing new. Omniscience sucks.*

So anyway, last week another hydro-bomb test blasted my reef home into anchovy liqueurs till ow, I woke with a mammoth hangover. Fucko McSucko—can't a B-flick stingray get a few eons' sleep? Don't you clam-butt fuckers have nothing better to do? Nuke this, snuff that—this rerun's getting old and I'm not. 'Cause mwah ha ha—I'm eternal! One of the perks of being—you guessed it—a Hello Devilfish! Meaning a ten-story plus-sized stingray—so cue up the soundtrack and let's get to wrecking! As angry cellos strum *duhn duhn duhhhh* while I slam a prune-blue tsunami over teensy waterfront hovels—Hello Devilfish! Did you miss me? I missed *you*—your twinkly factories spitting cadmium glitter—your sky-scrapers crammed with biped sausage—your day-cares chocked with human veal—whoa! So much to kill. And I'll trash stuff good, I promise—I can't wait to get tangled in sizzling power lines again. You can count on me—and I can only count to one. 'Cause my tail's my only digit—well, that and my fab stingray wiener—more about *that* traitor later. The road to pleasure is paved with squids. Only love can break your balls.

Should I invade downtown Tokyo again? Why not—it's where a beast rocks, a seething grid packed with human biomass. Though I gotta watch you suckers—you probably built new toxic kaiju splatter bombs I'll get croaked with on my next rampage— Hello War Crimes! But suddenly Tokyo's not enough—I need a bajillion trenches stacked with pony femurs and kitten skulls and rattlesnakes humping Barbie dolls—your basic suburban dream. Too bad everything forbidden's already been done— ask any Shriner. Still—I'll try to be anarchic, I promise—I'll roll penguins in cocoa and toss them to polar bears. I'll marry a snake and hide all the mice. Hah—the forbidden? I can't find it—someone hid it in their crusty slacks. Besides, evil is *so* corny—ever seen a Nazi hat? It will become dearer than former when I explain how I'm a—yep, you guessed it—Hello Devilfish! Let's say that a lot. Now the Devilfish what's me will obey all the customs. He's hoping pity and tears will scrub away his tawdry sins. Which are what—some pulped brats? A few charred bums? A lifetime of TV and cheap scotch? You need a fish to believe with.

So here I am, toppling skyscrapers with my stupendous tail while bodies tumble out like yellow salt—did I mention I'm a ginormous stingray? With nuke-proof iridium skin and I can spit green napalm jets—go monster chaos! Hah—watch me thrash through Tokyo, slicing charred arcs through factory prefectures, toasting strolling mommies into fried clumps—join our baby despair society! All you need is burnt milk. So why do I wreck stuff? Maybe I just dig your screams, that dumbstruck glance in death's grimy mirror. Except lately I'm more bored than your dad—burn this, smash that— I'm telling you, it gets like a job. A slave to fun's still a slave.

If it's later than former you're listening again, one hand on a stale beer and the other down your pants—Hello Erotica! I am a thing for much fun.

And if you're not me you're zip when I tell you—
kapow! How I churned streets into a creosote stew
burning brighter than firefly cum. Whee! Senseless
havoc totally *rules*—that clogged screech as scorched
toddlers burst into gummi poop—you gotta love
what you do. And I love torching you humps—I'm
God's chainsaw, her wired golem, the smile on
her power-drunk face—let's blaspheme! You need
to doom a world with more doom. And take to
limit while I chew babies or slash my razory tail
through noodle kiosks. What's with all the fucking
noodle kiosks?

Anyway, then I head for the shipyards—lots of
sparkly dioxin fun there—when I spot, alright—a
refinery! Till I sweat fire just cruising at that gas-
cracking plant, mmmm, those tangerine petrol pods
leaking sweet methane—this joint's gonna blow up
good. I was in pure form—my cobalt prick arcing
through cloud pussy, my tail snaking in spermy jet
streams till it lands *ka-thwhack* across that steel
nipple atop a reservoir tank. Let's drool like it's
Xmas! Especially when I tail-spank that spilled
naphtha into a fuel lotus, a hot blossom lit with

orange dread. While nearby worker humans squeal their usual *Eeek, help me Buddha* prayers till fire grills their minds away, yay! "How can we appease you?" one guy wails as his chest melts off. "Appease? Sorry," I smear him into dank paste, "don't know that word yet."

It's curious I even understand him—me talk Manglish, him Japanese. Hello Plot Flaw! With extra bored sauce. Hey, I did study some Asian lingo—a few Rosetta Stone phrase books floated past my coral lair. Still, my Japanese is pretty iffy—mostly shogun insults and geisha clichés. I know—let's just pretend everyone talks Manglish. I'm as lazy as fire! Really—this dock I'm wrecking ain't burning worth shit. And then bingo, it hit me—all I need is wings! Huge stingray wet ones to fan this baby inferno into a metastasized hell. I can haz Dada props? Not from you fuckers—you're born scared and die confused. And between the natal and omega bread of this greasy death sandwich—you look for *meaning*. You'd be better off looking for mayonnaise—Hello Devilfish! I giggle at your quandary. At night your over-amped brains sizzle like crude tumors while you grope through memory swamps, gorging on grief like some horrid unripe fruit. Smooshing you fuckers is a big large favor—Hello Panzers! You gotta fight for your Reich to party.

4

Brains are magic tricks done with meat. So watch out, Ms. Librarian! Don't put my book next to any other ones—I'll infect them. At night I pulse toxic blue on my dusty shelf—no one's safe. Not kiddie tomes, not 'tween soft-core, especially not dumb ethnic novels reeking with poverty. Their words hurt my liberty! All freedom is freedom for *me*—and ain't that the dream of the twenty-first century? So why am I here—to squash buildings, snort babies, chew grandmas into black drool? Amusing as all that is—I'm here to wipe out books. Erase them *completely*—make sure none are never nope wrote again. And how might a Devilfish do this? I'll invade every plot like a wild virus. Every time you read—it's about me! Grinning and wrecking and chewing stuff. *For Whom the Bell Tolls?* On Whom the Fish Rolls. *Moby Dick?* Moby Gone—now it's me roiling up that stinky sea! And Ahab's my love slave, mwah ha ha—dude does some pervy tricks with that whaler peg leg.

I am Happy Devilfish with an Amazon profile! You got Harlequin romances with steroid dudes and bustier chicks smirking on cheap covers? Wait— what's that *stingray* doing in the foreground? And why's he the bellhop at our assignation hotel? Don't tip the fucker, he's pretty clumsy. Eeek, watch out for his stinger—fucko, where'd my arms go— Hello Devilfish! I'm like a chunk of iced radium in your party mojito—hear my pulsing glow? Bzzzrp, bzzzrp—I'll kill everything. It's my nature, not my fault, wah. Mwah ha ha—self pity is the key to evil. *Poor me* is the gist of most pogroms.

I'm death on a stick—for all your leisure needs. Hello Devilfish! I'm a product for a thing you're not, you wuss. And you will say to a fey ray—how's it hanging? Low and inside, my brutha. Hmmm, so what next? I know—let's have a backstory! First off— what birthed me? Let's just pretend I leaped from a dead guy's brain—the same croaked fool who's name's on this book. T'was a night riddled with stars and mai tais—the fucker was in his Hawaiian mode back then. He'd moved lock, stock, and Mustang to some barren Kona reef seeking mana and cheap weed. What he really found—besides centipedes, leprosy and meth—was me! Smashing right out of his skull one humid night. He was pacing around his skanky motel room—his mortgage collapsed even faster than his marriage—when I burst through his brain pan.

"What the fucko?" he yelled.

"Hello Devilfish!" baby me shrieked, "let's say bad words!"

"You are *not* my baby," he muttered. Then he either drank or watched TV—hah—Mr. Lord of Lit. "Hi, Daddy," I squirmed around his suitcase, "let's write taboo memoirs!"

"I could *use* you," he narrowed those cagey eyes, "let's see. A plot about a young guy—no, not too young—"

"Extra bad words!" I chirped.

"Maybe set in Havana," he paced, "with a girl— I mean a woman, can't call them girls, and—"

"Mofo bad words that aggro the bitches!" I writhed my luscious blue bod on orange shag. Who puts orange shag down anymore? Even Commies won't touch it. I touched a tiny Commie. "Come on," I brushed him with my baby wing, "let's write evil blather."

"You talk the naxty pretty good," he smiled, "but there's my black friends, my Asian pals—and what if Chick Inc. gets wind of my apostasy—"

"Shriners fucking preteens!" I screamed. Uh oh—was I too subtle for him? Better ramp it up. "Midgets with wop sauce!"

"A novel about Tourette's?" he sneered. "It's been done."

"You're a coward," I twitched my stinger, "I'm sick of your prattling—you used to be *fun*. Why don't you Google your pen name again?" And that's when I crashed through patio glass and escaped—why hang with this fool? That twit was doomed to die unread and unfucked—and me? Mwah ha ha—I want to bathe in bad grammar, drink kitten milkshakes, coat myself with cheetah jism and rape the weeping sky—Hello Ambition! All your disgust are ours.

5

Tonight I wrapped my rubbery tail around a smokestack, ripped it up it and wrote in blood and memory. Your blood, my memory— Hello Devilfish! I wish I narrated stuff better—how scorched rice paddies curdle into mud soup with crow croutons, how torched skyscrapers melt like steel dildos—it's been sappy fun! You need a deity to laugh at. And you will say to God—hey fucktard! Who makes leukemia and cake in the same universe? She never answers—she? Hah—of course God's a chick. Who else goes all boo-hoo sentimental while snuffing their own spawn? She's like those hags that shake their baby apart and then plead post-nasal depression. God kills us 'cause she loves us! It's the logic of beaten dogs.

Let's say mild things—my prankster brain demands applause! As my bricky pen scribbles dirt ideograms about crime and lust and regret—regret's the most fun. You get to do evil shit and then oops, OMG, sorry, didn't mean it—I'm the prince of mad trauma. Especially when I stagger like some pregnant eggplant through chaotic muck, one stingray wing stirring streets into whirlpools and the other clutching dank hope. I hope there's more stuff to wreck—is that too much to ask? More twinkling death shooting like licorice rays from my raving tail? More piles of split pelvises with baby gravy on top? A hint of lime and matricide would spice things up nice. Plus maybe a svelte stingray chick to share my opulent wrack, her lips frothing down my fiery prick, our flanks gilded with spit and spunk as we smash through night at the speed of dawn—Hello Porn! When you make up stuff make it sexy.

But in real life I was still crushing that industrial wharf, shattering docks into splinter stew and gulping burnt workers like prole marshmallows. Till I spit their tongues out into a yelping confetti pile and drooled fire until my bod morphed into a gigantor blue flare. I am the light of the lost! Mostly lost limbs. But pure chaos is sort of comforting—you stop worrying about Facebook. No wonder some pimply reject buys a gun-show TEC-9 and lights up the nearest madrasa—hey, *you* try living with a flaming brain. And mine crackled as I toyed with the few biped chumps still alive, herding them from that dock's edge to a seared parking lot where their feet boiled off in gurgling tar. Onward toe-less soldiers! And then—hee hee—something tickled my flanks.

Yowza—was it my awesome fantasy stingray girl? I hope she brought liquor, some viscous rum that'll peel the paint off our skulls. We are having the sweet nougat life—join us in group-time flavor! Or battle-field furor—'cause fucko, what's tickling me is missiles! Shot from tube batteries hid in the trees. Everything's always hid in the trees—one rocket even smacks into my squinting eye! Not that it hurts me—you can't kill a Devilfish with heat-seeking tin—but it annoys the pure crap out of me. And also solves tonight's entertainment—'cause where there's rockets there's grunts nearby. Alright—let's make a screaming camouflage omelet! From that hilltop drill corps I smooshed into a brave and greasy puddle. Will these fuckers never learn? Remember, kids—violence never wins! It just levels things out.

Mwah ha ha—it was mondo glorious, a pop-art potpourri dripping runny gusto, my reeling wings and tail slaking the mud with jumbled bods and tanks and the lone kitchen truck—I am a blue baker of sobbing dough! Plus it's way mass even more fun watching humans panic—as those outgunned grunts fled like a beached wave, daubing the dirt with smeared dreams. A few loony infantry chumps even managed to sneak back and pop off a few mortars till I crushed them into the mothering dirt. What a waste—of my time! I can't bother with these sloppy hicks—I got an entire megapolis to destroy! Exactly—so I just simply charred that whole forest into oak toast, slicing hilltops off with my radiant wings while spit-bombing birds like fried comets. Whoever invented death had a kid's sense of humor—look, Mom—the cat farted and died! And then mmm, I sniffed big sugar. Was it pussy? Cash? Ferrets in lingerie? Nope—I smelled caramel corn. And also heard a lone calliope tooting out some goofy Souza tune—meaning there's gotta be a carnival nearby. Alright! 'Cause nothing spells brunch like boiled clowns.

6

Y ou can bone a steak but not your mom. And maybe I can bone Big Lit by subtly invading books. We'll start with some twentieth-century classics—Hello *CliffsNotes*! First off, let's trash *A Farewell to Limbs* by Zelda Hemingway—this honker about some castrated dude from a war. See what I mean? Lose a wang, gain a plot point. Anyway, this all happens in Paris—you can tell from the creepy yellow buildings. Someone's gotta clean this dive up—maybe I should just char it into Vichy rubble. But where's the boffo fun in that? And what am I doing in Paris anyway? I'm not gay or a poet, mwah ha ha—what's the diff? And why is my ray snout, ow, jammed into this teensy apartment? Where a skinny chick and fat dude wander around yammering fin de siècle nonsense. "I say, Count," some chick named Brett snarls, "do pour us some bubbly."

"Isn't she great?" the Count guffaws. Who guffaws anymore? "Huh? What?" I sputter fire, "huh?" And why am I hanging with these boozers? You need to stroke a fish for his luck. "Jake—don't be a boor," Brett whines, "do find us some clean glasses."

"Very clean," the Count smiles.

"Extra clean," Brett adds.

"Who's Jake?" I wrinkle my wet face.

"Amazingly clean," the Count ripostes. "Hello Devilfish!" I scream and smear him across the sink. Plus who's Jake? "That wasn't nice," Brett sighs, "you *can* be a beast."

"Permission granted? Thanks!" I lunge away, smearing Paris into brick mâché. There's gotta be a Frenchy way to end this tome—I know—how about the Eiffel Tower? So I rip it up with my radiant tail, shake some wailing tourists off, tuck it under my wing and hump back to Brett's flat. "Where *is* that champagne?" that bitch snarls.

"Hey, baby," I poke that Eiffel tip through her window, "you dig shish kabob?"

"Hello Jake!" Brett backs up onto some silky divan. Hmmm—should I squash her into floor jelly? Or wear her skin like a scarf? Nah, I'll just prong her with this Eiffel thingy—*kabongggggg*! Goodbye Lost Generation—Hello Devilfish!

And Hello Slums—woo hoo! Meaning this hovel district I wandered into after gutting that army. I salute you Major Ruckus! Fucko yes—I've always hated these rotting shacks hewn from bored work. You need a Devilfish to set you comrades right— meaning me! I'm anger with a tail and mass attitude. Destroy the running dogs of subtlety! Or just the running dogs—like that slobbering pack of collies I gulped down. Mmmm—they tasted most alpha. And somehow also stunk from caramel corn—no, wait—that's from that carnival I meant to wreck. *Geeraa!* I'll confess all now—it was a night lit by clown hair. Where I thrashed toward that crispy popcorn stench, shredding car lots and freight trains into aluminum salad. And after torching another freeway into smack-up soufflé I reached my radiant goal. Meaning this classic slack midway riddled with disco prepubes and gawking rubes. So cute—even the tots were swearing when I crashed the turnstiles, yay! Hello Devilfish! See how I subtly warp the dynamic? Who cares about nostalgia or tits when some crazed stingray is thrashing everyone into luminous goo? I bring you the cannibal century. I am the god of hellfire. How's my branding?

Alright! It was juicy mayhem—carnies and marks scurrying under smashed tents, me ripping spines out till they twist like drowned worms, addled moms shrieking like always—sheesh. Get a life, mom! And maybe churn out a few more tykes—they pop like milky cherries, mmmm. I even cornered a few hipsters by the Squid-o-tron ride. Meaning that pink iron squid ride with curly tentacle cars—which hmmm, no one was riding. Maybe 'cause it stank like a mummy's cunt. Plus who makes a ride shaped like a squid? It was fuglier than Mormon porn. Bizarre— its suckers even twitched a bit when I churned those nearby hipsters into plaid hat paste—take that, beardy dudes! All your beatnik are ours. And then I heard that evil calliope again.

Churning out this horrid steamy *Baby Elephant Walk* schlock you fuckers play to get cheerful. I spit on your cheer with stingray napalm, *geeraa*! And then thrashed that calliope into sonic tin—now it can play *Baby Stingray Walk*! While meanwhile I squashed more midway bodegas, slathering my bod with bloody cotton candy till I looked like some undersea tampon. I even got still and totally silent awhile, hoping these marks might mistake me for another attraction—like that pink Squid-o-tron ride that was hmmm, slinking away. But then all that spun sugar on me began to fricking *itch*—so I schlepped into a nearby marina. Us stingrays love baths—especially in mercuric harbor spas. I am bluer than most Smurfs! I will always haunt your malls. Just like those steamy tentacles grappling the wet horizon—huh? Strange— somehow that iron Squid-o-tron came alive and moseyed into my harbor. Was it some mondo robotic wonder, some time-warp Terminator sent to snuff my sorry butt? Hah—my butt is never sorry—and what kind of hokey pink ride just ups and escapes? I mean besides youth and pussy.

7

My love—you are my love—never let go of our hopes and dreams. Now I'm confused—I want to be good but I crave victims. I have no pals—I'm lonely like dice in a church. So what to destroy next? Hmmm—how about this marina I'm already swimming in? Let's drum up some human kibble—Hello Devilfish! Be cheery with cheerful qualities. Anyway, so I'm slicing moored boats into fiberglass chili, la la la, smooshing bosuns and fleeing deckhands—when I spot a yacht trying to escape! Mwah ha ha—no one escapes the dapper Devilfish. Not when I swoosh out and waggle my fatal tail at some yacht hottie who screams "Eeek! Squidra!"

"Huh? No—I'm *Hello Devilfish!* See?" I tap her

chin with my tail barb, "Stingray! Devilfish! Plus I talk your hot language."

"Eeek! Squidra!" she howls again, her bikini butt trembling with fear—so natch I eat the silly bitch. Mmmm—she tastes like a baked wig. And while spitting her gallbladder out, ewww—I see that lurking Squid-o-tron ride munching people too! Fucko McSucko—that ain't no ride—it's an actual gigantor kraken! *Duhn duhn duhhhhh*—fucko! It's Squidra! She's like a nightmare beast from a nightmare—pinker than birth and squirmier than a nude junkie. Plus she's chowing down my victims—mine! I hate her like a thing. And you will say to a Devilfish, listen bub—you gotta kill stuff to own it. So grab a heart, put your ax in it, and listen to me babble! I'm a story with story ideas. And Squidra's my fugly problem! She moves like an armed pickle—plus she's got orange eyeball laser rays! Grrr, grrr—what a whup-ass weapon! Whoa—she just squints till her microwave vision shears through masts and skulls with surgical glitter—and also torches a huge welt across my left wing, ow. "Hello Mr. Demon Fish—glarb," she gulps a swimming helmsman, "I've been *watching* you."

"It's *Devilfish*, not demon fish—*geeraa!*" I roar, scaring some waves away, "and who *are* you?"

"The girl you're *meant* for," she bats her gummi eyebrows.

"Buzz off! Ow," I lick my burnt wing, "and get your own happy death farm! This is my Tokyo—mine!"

"You wish," Squidra flutters her seaweedy tongue, "come on, sweetie—let's make *love*." Whoa—she's obviously sicker than gangrened fudge—*love* her? I'd rather socially slay and eat her—but she's way huge! And sleek with gooey curves—she gives me urges like Elmer Fudd gets for Bugs Bunny in drag. Cunning pheromones were def out to trap me—biology's always lurking. Stupid biology—what's it ever made to brag about? Malaria and turkeys? Have a Coke and some pants again! With some fish-lust stew thrown in—the slop du jour I gagged on while gawking at my new honey—Squidra! Her tentacles like rain crawling through cyberspace—her curves flaring like wet jonquils—her eyes blinking with drunk baboon force—her suckers flexing like a billion lips—Hello Stalker! Hey, you try untying eight tentacles wrapped like demented bow ties around your gills. "Go *away*," I curl my bod into a blue-wing taco till she slides off.

"What's *your* problem," Squidra sulks, "you think I'm too fat?"

"What? Huh?" Fucko—where'd *that* come from? "You are freaking *whack*," I shove her, "shoo!"

"Do you like the band Foreigner?" Squidra crumples another mast into pine mush, "I love their version of "Urgent." *Urgent, dee dee dee, so urrrrrrgent*—urgent like *you*," she coos, "so gimme kisses!" Whoa—what's with girls? They creep up on you like commas. Let's have a marriage lifestyle—it's called Hubby Life. Just mix obsession and dumb smooches—add on a tiff about pay equity and some weak mimosas—and put that suburban muumuu *on*. "Vamoose!" I duck her searing eyeball rays. "Scram!"

"You think you're so *hot*," uh oh, Squidra's eyelids glow even oranger, "who made *you* king?"

"I'm always king—king hot pants!" I laugh, "*Geeraa!* Now am-scray."

"Some king," Squidra sneers, "you can't even talk romance to a *girl*," and whoa, now I def should flee.

She said *romance*! Plus *talk* and *girl*—words that stun your tongue like wasp pie. I'm a myth worth lying about! "You *know* you want me," Squidra puckers up. Uh oh—was it true? Did I actually lust after Squidra's nicotine-black beak, her red-lead mouth, her puss flexing like nude pudding—no wait, *that's* her mouth. Add on her retinal lasers crackling yachts into charred goop—fucko! Eyeball rays! Why ain't I got a sick weapon like that? Let's have a sulk with grump sauce.

It all started—wait, it started already—with me confused by harpy sex desire. Face it, bros—we're pussy-whipped mopes who'd follow a spayed poodle straight to hell—we've been bamboozled, chained to a smelly meme, a wet Death Star that sucks our jizz comets in. "*Adore* me," Squidra twines me with her Twizzler red tentacles, "I'm gorgeous!" You need to trick a ray into sex—Hello Devilfish! That goes without saying. So does doom—as Squidra flares like popped bubblegum when I giggle "Gorgeous? You look like God's snot ball." Awww, did I shun her girly lures? Good! 'Cause mwah ha ha—now she'll fight me, yay! I'm a lout worth scrapping with—just let me drool some starter fire, flex my stingray wings, prep my tail and *smoke* her. Maybe I can fuck and devour her afterward—sweet! True, she outmatches me—she's fatter than Kansas and just now scorched my other wing with her horrific mango Kool-Aid eyeball laser beams—but I spit big flame! My enemies will be lurid toast. But when I puke a napalm tsunami at that greedy cephalopod—she just surfs it back at me! Did I mention she's way colossal huge? Uh oh—I'm gonna get my wet butt stumped *good*.

8

Plots are for babies and geezers. At the end of the novel—Jesus gets the girl! After he punks the smug quarterback and saves the gator mascot from a handbag cabal. Bore me with sleep sauce! Really—you want little stories? How's this one—Death is your boss and Pain is your wife. It's a sitcom—Pain's dinner party goes awry when Death spills alum in the pizza dough. The laugh track's been looping for billions of years—Hello Devilfish! You can see why I need to destroy stuff. Hey, at least I got away from Squidra—'cause instead of tussling and losing, I just dove down some harbor channel. I can haz panic? And after cruising through this undersea Yakuza graveyard—a swaying garden of swelled bodies wrapped in leaky chains—I surfaced near night Tokyo. Alright! This was my Broadway, my Emmies, my Show of Shows—this neon pile spiked with weeping meat and estrogen. Meaning all the chicks I'd get to snarfle down! They're usually tastier than dudes—plus who wants a gazillion dicks in their mouth? I mean besides most guys from Montana.

And so har har, I lurked beneath a simmering tide, sniffing the lair of the land, calculating the Tetris parameters of which ripped skyscraper to stuff where. Oooo—this was the night I daydreamed about for snoring eons. As I flogged the sea with my engorged tail, gargled some fire and then—*geeraa*—rose like a blue ghost. Where I smooshed another wharf, mushing dockhands into a denim grease that I slid on into downtown. Let's make a grief smoothie! Start with fresh guts, then sprinkle with scared pee, girdles, Parcheesi boards, and sizzling lips. Now whip this mess into a blood frappe, pour into a milk truck and suckle it *down*. I am God's toddler! That fucker needs a parenting class.

Her kids are total monsters. *Geeraa!* That's my creamy motto—I sang it while spitting fire juice at that warbling crowd—you could make a porn compilation from my napalm money shots. Maybe even mix in some latex bustier foot-fetish action to market to the basement trolls. But right after crunching a few skyscrapers into rusty toast—when the elevators burst it's a human sashimi treat—I halted in that smoking wreckage. Something was def wrong. Whoa—all this senseless devastation—all this wanton, useless cruelty—it ain't cruel enough! I came to wipe hope from the map, not play urban developer. You bet, mayor—after we level Pimp Town, we'll build a Williams-Sonoma Macchiato Hut!

Hey, I know—sometimes Art gives you freaks hope. Why is beyond me—no matter how you paint your grave it's still dirt. So *duhn duhn duhhhhh*—let's destroy Big Art! With nonsense and violence and beauty— you gotta toss in beauty to fool the chicks—Hello Devilfish! I really can't say that enough. So let's raze some galleries, yay! As I trashed this Noho district with my crazed tail, jabbing aesthetes into shriveled lumps and whipping Brutalist lithos into boho gruel—hah! Till blazing patrons screeched around like schizo pinballs—that'll give them something to Art about. But I soon got bored with smooshing all this kitsch—Art croaks on its own. With big and frosty twitches! Plus why am I babbling about Art—I'm here to kill books! I'll kill them to death. I'll squish presses with my heavy wings and scrawl poems in lit petrol—I'll yelp till the cowering stars shoot their lumen loads—I'll scream delish nonsense till you bipeds agree that I'm King Lit! You should respect my pants and agree. Hah—I can already hear the Squidras of the world bitching—*That dumb fish can't even talk right, fer chrissakes—and what's with all the sex boasting? He thinks he's the Marquis de Cod*— Hello Devilfish!

But hmmm—what Lit pit to raze first? Should I pulp libraries into sans-serif mulch? Or maybe just torch the whirring server farms where e-Pulp hides in pixel shame? All good and rude fun—but if you really want to throttle belles lettres, just wipe out liquor. A sober poet is a minor poet. So I sniffed around till I nosed in on the brewery district—which natch was next to the slummiest slums. Hey, you gotta give the serfs *some* amnesia drug—either liquor or morphine or cable news—otherwise they'll wise up to their fucked prole reality. Hello Trotsky! I'll show them some guerilla dialectics, mwah ha ha—just wait till their precious goofer juice sloshes into those thirsty sewers. Plus while I wrecked their booze factories I could get sloshed myself. Bash your brains with bongo wine! Me, I craved a colossal drink—maybe a spinal-fluid Manhattan with a speared elephant garnish. Hello AA! I def need a better sponsor.

Anyway, after a few klicks of schlepping wings over crumpled wharves and kebobbing Datsuns with my gourmet tail—I found the land of hard drink. And whoa, these were titanic liquor-cracking plants, chocked with pot-still toxins and funky Midori—yee haw! Bro, no one gets hammered like the Japanese—they never really did Puritanism here. Nope—they went straight from grubbing feudal poverty to pomo industry—with a little six-year diversion into Nanking and germ warfare. Happy Sneaky Emperor—Hello WWII! And Hello Double Boilermaker—as I made a fish beeline at some ethanol tanks, slicing them open with my scalpel tail and guzzling all the unaged booze. Which must've been 150 proof 'cause whoa—I got bonkadonk drunk. Yes! This was *so* worth all the swimming miles to get here—to go pure hillbilly with my snout jammed in the world's hugest Martini. Hah—that swill made me as crazed as a bipolar shark.

You talking to me? Mwah ha ha—I felt pure murder syrup ladling my veins, roid rage bathing my nerves till in my eyes glowed into green amperes. Whoa—I need to think up sicker torments for these biped mofos. I'll rip pregnant chicks into caesarian stew. I'll mentor a Three Stooges gender-studies course. The only problem is—whenever I summon chaos—it always appears! As *kaboom* a gigantor pink kraken rears up, crushing mash pits into sugar dust. Uh oh—goofy Squidra done found me! She is both twit and silly—and stinks worse than a Romanian hostel. "Where's my lover boy?" she screeches. What a pest! I hate her like stuff. Grrr, grrr—let's have a grrr. It's monkey ripe with best flavor—Hello Devilfish! I'm a strange one.

9

Mwah ha ha, nobody's safe—my venom has seeped into your dreams! All your skull are ours. What's my toxin? This prickly stinger goop I inject in your minds—that's it, shhh, let it take effect. How's it work? It already has—what do you scribble about? Gollums? Hobbits? Hunky spies with satyriasis? Then I've succeeded—in making you forget about hot buttered death! Hello Rubes—I got you to ignore the only sure thing in your flimsy biped lives—me! And my splendid destructo tail—a butt whip made from equal parts chaos, boredom, and nonsense. For all your humane needs. I can see you at your teensy iPads, texting "*I am King Tweet!*" while war and famine and Visa cards rain on your tawdry Formica huts. Try and type *me* away, muthafuckas—whee! My cunning is crueler than Muslim bees.

Let's obey my sparkling urges—like the urge to evade Squidra! Meaning that pink hump whose tentacles whir night into a stardust slurpee that ripples across my skin. Huh? Tentacles? I probably should pay more attention—but where's the large fun in that? And my fun was guzzling cheap corn liquor and stumbling around on floppy wings all totally bozo drunk. Maybe I should I limit myself to fifty gallons a day—join our happy rum lifestyle! Just be sure to aim your puke—I sure didn't—when I hurled cheap booze, human tracheas, and some odd tractor I'd gobbled all over a distillery roof. I still fondly remember the screams—mostly coming from Squidra! "Helloooooo, Mr. Devilfish," that amorous cephalopod writhes her bootylicious tentacles, "look at you, you bad-boy drunk."

"*Geeraa!*" I spit napalm at her nose. Or I think it's her nose—who can tell with squids? "That's not nice," she sulks. So what? My hate is powerful and evil—it's evil and powerful! My hope, you are weirder than gophers. And why is Squidra crashing my kill-fest?

She looks so pink—she's very pink! And beyond fugly.
Ewww—what if she wants slobbery kisses and
smoochy hugs? I can't deal with horny chicks tonight.
Or later. Or ever. Plus what's she expect—congratu-
lations on her Tokyo debut? Raw humping slappy
action? A chill pill wouldn't hurt—as that daft kraken
sweeps her orange eyeball rays over distillery roofs till
workers howl and stumble out. She even gathers a
bunch in one twisty tentacle and thrusts that
squirming mess in my face. "Here's a bouquet!" she
chirps, "because we're meant to *be*."

"Meant to be what?" drunk me giggles.

"We're like *The Days of Wine and Roses*," Squidra
chews up a few dudes, "ever seen that movie?"

"I don't watch movies," I sneer, "or my weight. Or
dumb girls."

"Looky," she sashays closer, "I dressed *up* for you."
Meaning she'd twisted melted fiberglass and tattered
sails into this weird chiffon skirt. "Do you like my
couture?" she tilts like a bloated toy. "No—you're
naxty!" I roar. Oops—some girls just don't like direct
insults. Especially squids of oozy tonnage. "You—
you've hurt my *feelings*," Squidra drops her corpse

bouquet. Where one worker wriggles out, gurgles nonsense and falls off the dock and drowns. Will he be honored in song and saga? Nuh uh—and me neither if I keep up this drunken grump. "I said," Squidra gets in my blue face, "you hurt my *feelings*."

"Then don't have any, you bimbo—*geeraa*!" I roar at the flaccid heavens. It was a night full of dark and stuff. Where I'm reckless with booze action—Hello DTs! "Fuck off," I snarl like barbed wire. "But I made reservations at McDonald's," Squidra sulks. So what again! Does she expect me to tag along and chew pimpled McWorkers? Human junk food gives me serious cramps. "You'd *better* love me," Squidra growls. "Um, sure," I flatten my ears. Uh oh—is Mr. Devilfish giving up? Nuh uh—like any true grifter I'm just stalling for time. Let's chew my doleful boner! I'm your extra vague pal.

I even mused about maybe just raping Squidra, pinning her with my dank wings while I drink her drooling fear. Mwah ha ha—I am Devilfish, destroyer of moods! But she's way stronger than me and might just chomp my wiener off! It's a weenie that deserves more history! You gotta do something to pass the time. I know—let's have a delusion! Mine was I could brush Squidra's crush off—as she cranked up her laser eyeball rays and made grim faces at me. Alright—me and her are gonna have an old-timey kaiju B-flick smack down! Hey, it beats porking her— she's a fricking squid! Fucko—she looks like a bum's glove stuck in a Coke bottle. Hello Product Spill-in!

Anyway, then she totally whipped my blue butt. With screams and lasers and flailing kaiju pink parts—those were mostly hers—as we grappled and squashed pipes into an industrial wasteland. That we wasted! As crushed trucks and valves and factory glass got whipped into a gray pudding that slathered our wrestling bods. *Geeraa*! Your angst is not welcome. Neither were Squidra's blows—as she whomped me across a parking lot, crisping my flanks with her orange laser rays—ouch! Why do bad things happen to worse stingrays?

I can haz sex burger? Anyway, we ended up tussling in some lab district, a steaming grid of hormone tanks and fetal slop troughs. I didn't even get to gnaw any fleeing science nerds as Squidra tossed me at some purple tank covered with biohazard memes. I

think it said HGH or Human Growth Hormone—
which would def explain what happened next. I am a
proud slob warrior! Fucko—nothing's worse than getting beat by a girl—not even love with hot dumb
sauce. Plus somehow I'd got my radiant tail jammed
in that tank ladder—I couldn't even sting her! Even
writhing around and howling didn't help—and it
usually does. Ask any stripper. Plus I didn't have my
mace or rape whistle on me—so I decided to play
dead. But Squidra didn't fall for my fish corpse act.
"You coward," she hissed, "fight like a man."

"You mean a human man?" I laughed. "And what—
get smooshed by the millions? Screech around with
flaming hair?" As Squidra closed in for the kill,
flexing up on two tentacles and thrashing me with the
night-spangled rest. Till I crashed through that tanker
roof and into milky bio-muck. Where I fainted in
HGH glop and wondered—hmmm—where *was* that
extra-bacony sex burger?

10

"**O**w—*geeraa*—fricking *ow*," I muttered awake in the viscous depths. *WTF* methinks—was this a comatose daydream? Sheesh—my brainpan could've conjured up something more risqué than drowning in beige sex lube. 'Cause that's what it smelled like—let's have a sex! With garters and sneaky guilt. But coma or no, for some reason I couldn't breathe liquids no more—which makes no sense for a stingray fish. Instead I choked and swam up through that lewd goo—my wing thrusts felt amazingly lame—and surfaced with a *kerplop* on the rim of that smashed HGH tank. Ick—human growth hormone tastes naxtier than braised feet with broccoli. And I ought to know.

"*Geeraa!*" I howled at the smarmy heavens—except whoa, I sounded kind of pipsqueak. Never mind vocal vanity—I must fight the stinky Squidra! Except that freaking squid was nowhere in sight—and everything in sight was, um—bigger. Way mass bigger. What the fucko—had the whole world shot gonzo steroid juice when I fainted? Nuh uh—the earth was the same boring size. It was me what had shrunk—Goodbye Devilfish! Mostly 'cause I'd morphed into something way worse than any hobo, bug, or homeless virus. I'd turned—*duhn duhn duhhhhh*—human! Eeek! And then beaucoup more *eeeks* when I slogged out of that deforming HGH goo and into a Squidra-charred landscape. Hello Changeling!

But this biped bod's gotta be some rogue hallucination—how could something so macabre happen to moi? I can't see it going down—mostly 'cause my new human bino-vision was totally squiggly. Really—both eyes on the same side? You fuckers are flounders. And I floundered good when I tried standing up—and flapped smack on my new nose, ow. And then stood up on—you're kidding me—legs? Who created these wobbly honkers? Seems God was drunk in shop class again—how else explain toes? And even worse are elbows—mine were already scuffed bloody from crawling on bashed cement. Hey, I was a stingray just moments ago—we don't do the walking—I keeled over my first four tries. Let's flop like brave waffles! But panic's the mother of tactics—and I had to get gone. 'Cause any minute that freak kraken would swarm back to date, mate, and polish me off. Let's polish one off for Jesus! He's nailed up and can't do it himself.

Anyway, I managed to sloppy drunk-walk through fresh wreckage, stopping now and again to marvel at my new skin. 'Cause even the wind hurt it! You bipeds are weaker than baby trout—whiny, murderous trout who yank strange beliefs from your scaly butts. But even weirder than just fragile skin was its color— mine was dusky blue. Nice hue—except everyone else is yellow! I wonder if the Japanese shun folks that don't fit in. With a little ash and ink I could probably pass for black. Then I could kill Big Lit 'cause it *owes* me—Hello Quotas! All your guilt are ours.

All your shame too—as I slunk through sodden alleys and into packed Tokyo. Where mutherfucking ow—I kept bumping my blue butt on brick walls. Probably 'cause I swayed like a used noodle—hey, it's how us rays move. Or did before I morphed into a shivering human dolt. Why shivering? 'Cause I just heard Squidra's mucus trill echoing off smashed girders. Grrr, grrr—this city is *my* holocaust! Mine! Or it was—now I've gone biped, turned teensy, traded my nighthawk mind for a skull crammed with gods and dead mommies. You twerps call this dink lump a *brain*? And the stringy stuff on top—that's hair? Really? And why's it already in a crude bouffant? Hello Jack Lord! Maybe I should style the other curls down there where—eeek! My fab weenie done shrunk! To about the size of a cheap blue cigar. Hah—what a piece of pie man is—how stupid in brooding—how like a TV that only gets reruns—a poor crusty donut who smears frosting on the stage. Anyway, to recap—I'm now human, bluer than a drowned baby's twat and stark barking naked—no wonder everyone dodged me. Especially when I lurched at them with my spaz limbs and screeched *geeraa*! I was crippled, clumsy, and slow—I can be Walmart greeter?

11

I can haz McJob! So I'm a biped—now what? Should I turn wage slave and raise a drooling family? Not a bad idea—kick-start some tender human larva—and then devour them, yay! All your Donner Party are ours. It's the only way I'll cop any decent grub—these puny hands are worthless! They're as weak as newborn crabs. Awww, come on—was my groovy Devilfish bod really history? Really? I'll never demolish another megapolis? Never chew more orphans into groaning salsa? Whoever dreamed up civilization was stone nuts. Did I really swap a lifetime of lethal bliss for this—a pudgy gut and silly knees? Apparently so—Hello Bitch Fest! And goodbye nutsack—my new human balls barely swing! Was it really just yesterday I boiled out of bleak seas, my carbide bod arcing like a sleek blue boner? Back then I fucked the sun into a jillion spermy splinters—now I stumble around like some gimp Muppet. Are we insane yet? Hold on to your winkie and find out. And then—thank you Allah—I saw a gas station.

It's like they say—when in Rome don't eat relics and when in Tokyo blow shit up. And when I waddled past a beer-lit minimart—and spied that leaking gas pump—I let loose with a wild *geeraa!* A cry what once torched the sky with lurid fire—and now only stank the joint up with ape breath. "Hey, you—naked blue gaijan!" some pump jockey shambles over. "Go back to gaijan town!"

"Gaijan? What?" I puzzle. Oh, right—*gaijan* are foreigners. And blue pyro nude ones def count. "Leave now!" he brandishes a broom. Great—I've devolved into some wuss any Ronin janitor can kung fu with cheap housewares. Hello Impotent Rage! Meaning I'd better duck that flailing broom and figure out how to snuff him. It's what a Devilfish does! Even a morphed monkey one. Look, I don't tell *you* how to work—let's have a sick lifestyle! It's called Lifestyle

Job. "Blue gaijan!" that pump jockey spits at me, "shoo!" Fucko—what's he so ticked about? I ain't even blown anything up yet. I can haz glory?

Anyway, so I'm batting that swooshing broom away with my useless arms—*useless* is a totally human word—when aha! I spy a dropped Bic lighter. What sort of skull-fucker strews lighters around a gas station? Some biped with a death wish, mwah ha ha— so let's grant it! As I smack a pump handle loose till it spews yummy gas. Hey, someone's gotta commit— meaning me when I duck manic bushido straw, flick that lighter on, toss it at fumes and run. Till I stop a half block away and dance a crude jig—mostly wagging my junk like a tail—when this Girl Scout giggles. At what—that delish petrol fireball? That crispy gas jockey screeching around? Nope. "Hot dog! Blue hot dog!" she points at my bare dangler. "Look, Mommy—I can see his *thing*."

Oh right—pants! I not wearing any. "Wait, I can explain," I mutter as that crowd closes in, their wicked fish knives already out—to slice off my pervy balls! What—really? You guys don't bone your own kids? Get with the program—nature's just a galactic prick spewing wet stars into raped space—Hello Devilfish! I can see why no one carpools with me. Plus eeek, don't chop my eensy human peener off—I might need it! Seems it's a monkey spark plug for revving guilt and hate. Like just now when—who else—Squidra shows up! Screeching bon mots and choking street-cars into bloody rust—she probably spotted that gas station blaze and *knew* it was me. "Mr. Demon Fish— where *are* you—" she gurgles while the crowd goes *Oooooo* and gawks up at her schlumping rump. Which was my cue to um, disappear. Note to self—stay away from Girl Scouts, fish knives, and hulking squids. And while you're up maybe grab some pants too.

12

What doesn't kill you almost kills you—Hello Devilfish! Today class, we're gonna decon- struct the cancer narrative—it's gnarly chemo fun! Jeez, I hate these sappy fables where Betty finds a breast lump and becomes—a better person! Hah—what she actually morphs into is a chop-shop freak—with a narrative woven from very wooly clichés. Hope it keeps her toasty—who's gonna date some hag with one fun bag? These god-awful cancer books frost my balls—all these slipshod tomes about battling for your teensy life—with an uplifting message! Listen, fighting the Big C is like wrestling a freight train— *I approached the diesel beast like a friend, not an enemy. Maybe it had something to teach me—a lesson in love and laughter? Or maybe how to rip a skull into screaming paste.*

Hello Stage 4! All your squamous are ours. Who cares about your spiritual journey—how enlightened was that bacon you scarfed at breakfast? Maybe Mr. Pig thought that slaughterhouse hook was gonna lift him to heaven too. A heaven filled with knives and bright screams—Hello Devilfish!

Lover, you're not my lover, shhh. Never give up on our hopes and dreams. But for sure give up on trouncing Squidra—she was in manic chaos mode. My chaos, mine! Though hopefully some Stryker jets would make puréed calamari from her ginormous butt any second. Hey, it ain't the 1950s—you bipeds can pretty much snuff *anything.* Except a Hello Devilfish! Who'd probably better skedaddle—'cause here they come! Three stealth bombers that slice night into sonic pasta—and then plop like graphite meatballs when Squidra zaps them with her orange eyeball lasers, bzzrt, bzzrt, her suckers pulsing like firefly swarms, her tentacles lashing out like a pink asterisk. Whoa! I can haz death burger?

Cool—could Squidra actually pull this off? Could she wreak total Armageddon? Let's hear more twinkly noises! As smacked hotels shred into glass flak under

Squidra's FX tentacles—grrr, grrr—she's stealing my rampage! Mine! Hmmm—so why am I standing here like a dazed popsicle while doom and mayhem rain around me? Um, 'cause wherever I am is where doom and mayhem reign. 'Cause eeek—a chubby squid is after me! Just me. Honest. Plus fucko—she just spotted me again! I can tell by her goofy grin. "Here, Demon Fish," she coos and *schlump—schlump—schlump* oozes closer till I feel her septic breath. "That's bizarre," she sniffs me, "you're a walker—but you *smell* like him. Explain."

Hah—could I ever explain her whack passion? I doubt it—I left my DSM-VI at home. But maybe Squidra *was* my fated mate—what was that my mom used to screech? *You get the spouse you deserve—now help me devour your father.* She yelled that right after she bit daddy's head off, him thrashing like a tased frog, all us stingray spawns lapping up his muddy blood—memories, memories. Whee! I'm a thing you should rub. A lot. While I'm on my back. No, lower—hah—as low as me crawling through a drainpipe right now. Why? 'Cause evil Squidra's on my trail! I got a date with death—and death's a total porker. "Come here, leetle changeling," Squidra tosses riprap at my drainpipe to ferret me out—eeek! Uh oh—am I headed like my whipped dad for an undersea buffet? Or even worse—torrid nooky? "Hey—hey *you*," Squidra blocks my drainpipe escape with her slinky tentacles, "why you smell like my boyfriend?"

"I'm not your boyfriend—*geeraa*!" I scream what should be napalm spit—but just drools out like bum juice. "Aha," Squidra's oozy eyeball seals my drainpipe, "it *is* you! You've turned into a toy!"

"We don't want you playing with us," I scuttle back asswards.

"You're *shrunk*," she slips a tentacle around me.

"Um no, ma'am—you're mistaken—no Devilfishes here," I hug pipe rust, "Mr. Stingray died. He dead! Big time fun dead!"

"I dunno," she peers closer, "you sure talk like him. Same dumb Manglish crap."

"He—he's gay! Eeep," I squeak when she squeezes me. "That's why I smell like him! We did the naxty in the sauna. Happy prick invasion life!"

"No way he's gay," Squidra giggles, "not with *his* grooming. You seen his ear hairs? They're longer than surfboards."

"If you hate him so much,"—why am I arguing with a fish?—"then why you stalking him?"

"Love is mysterious," Squidra coos.

"No it ain't! *Geeraa!*" I screech like a jailed mynah, "plus he hates you! Icky girl, icky!"

"You're a feisty changeling," Squidra squints closer—ewww, I can even see her slimy chin wrinkles. "But how'd you turn human? Wait—we were near some bio-factory—goddamn it," she bitches when a rogue fire truck bonks her fin, "don't these fuckers ever stop?" They do when she slaps that truck into the guzzling sky—and hee hee, drops me onto that gore-slicked street. "Bye!" I laugh, skittering knees and hands across a squid-wracked wasteland. What—I should stick around and fight—with this useless human bod? Hah—if fate will slay me, why, fate may chase my blue butt. Hello Devilfish! I got nothing to add.

ook—I really, really want to end Big Lit. I'm not kidding—join our censor lifestyle! It's called Censor Life. But how to really, really end Lit? Every time you harass the wordy sucker—it co-opts you! You go slasher, sexist, gross-out, nonsensical— the meta-narrative simply *absorbs* you. I never met a narrative I didn't hate. Next thing you know, some beardy dude is using *you* as a plot! *Ahem, yes—my new book's about a poem-hating stingray. He's a sensitive little putz.* Here's what I've tried—you tell *me* if it worked. Crush presses, gulp pulp mills, chow down authors and critics? Lit goes ebook and mob democratic— now everyone's a writer! With vague and boring needs. And don't get me raving about gender skir- mishes—dude writers were dumb enough—now we got a billion chicks picking their memory scabs! *My sex-ed teacher ignored me. Grandpa spurned my bondage forays.* Chicks live in the past like cranky fossils—Hello Devilfish! I'm big fun in a small can.

Anyway, the skinny is I dodged raging Squidra by sprinting through some foundry prefecture, this pomo maze of smokestacks and girders and incomprehensible pictographs squirming on torn ads. This was def a Buraku district—everywhere stank from fish butts and despair. What are Buraku? They're Japan's untouchables—the caste that for millennia burned corpses and slaughtered pigs and ate all the carp guts. Tokyoites call them *sluckers*—don't ask how *that* slur arose—and only a gaijan like me would even admit they exist. Who cares? Let them figure their own karma out—I was blue and needed pants. I looked like a Level 3 Smurf pedophile.

Let's have the pop reference! Truth be told—and it won't—I was still more ray than human in my morphed biped mind. For starters, I couldn't really walk—staggering like a drugged shark don't count— and I still wiggled my arms like fish wings. Nothing to see here, folks—just another blue rube doing the

funky chicken. I can haz James Brown? And then—
ahem—there's the power line incident. Which went
down when I lurched and keeled through goofy streets
and nearly tripped on *duhn duhn duhhhhh*—some
downed power lines! Sizzling and writhing in voltaic
knots. More of Squidra's oeuvre, no doubt—us kaiju
love to plow through watt towers, amp cables, cathode
clots—anything that squirms like ghost ramen when
you wreck it. Plus some voltage poles were still
standing! Almost as crooked as me when I ran at
those dangling wires—force of habit, gotta smash
them—waggling my arms and screaming my cute
lungs out. *Geeraa*! I think I woke maybe a half hour
later with black sparks tattooed across my chest. "Blue
mansu, blue mansu," some meter maid shook me,
"you alright?"

"Get lost," I snarled and lurched up. And what's
with the *blue mansu*? Oh right—my skin. *Blue Mansu
Group* is this Tokyo lounge trio that smear their heads
with cerulean goo and play jazz marimbas—I swear I
almost heard them in my scorched eardrums. So
that's it—really? I can't even eat simple voltage anymore? Wah—why is the world against me? I just

wanna kill it—and maybe get some pants. Which was mondo easy—I just found a wrecked alley and stripped the nearest Squidra victim who didn't poop his drawers. Plus I copped a cool aloha shirt too— I've always wanted to smear Honolulu back into the roiling sea. I can haz nice Hawaiian Punch?

Maybe a soggy mac-salad plate too—I was that famished. It was minutes since I last ate—and us Devilfish need mass grub. So what do these human-oids chow down on, anyway? They ain't devoured each other for centuries. Luckily—or un—my new monkey nostrils drew me into this gigantor fish mart. Which wasn't even panicked about looming Squidras yet—Tokyoites learned decades ago to work around whatever Gamera or US Air Force Corps rained death on their ducking skulls. Nope, they just kept on gutting trout and slurping eels—even as her whop-ping tentacles smeared the horizon into cement scrapple. Still, crowding into that fish bazaar *would* be pretty dumb. Yep—that'd be me, staggering into that packed perch mall, elbowing geezers and fishwives aside—and plunging my snout into a cart of butch-ered hake. "Yum," I chewed up scales and gills that crackled like martyred locusts—till I'm yanked from my gory banquet! "Get out of here, thief!" some fish-monger raised his cleaver.

"What you gonna do," I giggled, "eat me?"

"Stealing! You're stealing!"

"Sheesh, calm down," I snatched a huge hake up, "or I'll have to fish-slap you."

"Evil blue gaijan—go away!" he hissed. Good thing I didn't know my own strength—cause it sucked! I could barely tap him with that clumsy hake. But I did muster enough entropic motion to smack my hand into his blurring cleaver—which chopped off my pinky! "You're kidding," I stared at the gushing stump, "*red* blood?"

"I'll kill you—thief!" he raised that glinting cleaver again! While that thronged market chanted "Thief—thief—" and I did some quick math. Hmmm, let's see—Squidra to the south, lethal monger to the west—better head east. Where? To the slums and hovels where the ragged stingrays go. Hello Devilfish! Won't you take me to Buraku town?

et's looking for tropes! Mwah ha ha—today I'll infest this hoary abolitionist potboiler called *Uncle Tom's Houseboat*. With a Grade-A silly plot starring halibut slaves and incomprehensible massas. Seems what the Yankees really stole was their consonants—*I doan' know nothin' about birthin' no perch*! Anyway, our tale opens with Hammerhead Legree dragging a gigantor slave fish to de auction block. It's Mama Stingray! She ripples with calico fat. "Please," she moans, "forsake to sell us down that fetid river."

"Mwah ha ha," Simon rubs his fins, "we's gwine to sell you *an'* yo baby ray—bring that buck fish in heah."

"Oh Mother!" I wail, twisting my chains and punching my gigantor blue tail through a mast.

"Dear matriarch," I weep flaming snot, "they shall sell my precious bod!"

"My God," some tuna matron sniffs, "can't that ray-tard say *anything* in patois?"

"Hurry up with dis piscine oppression!" Hammerhead Legree spits tobacco juice at Mama Stingray. Why not? She's a dead thing on paper like me—Hello Devilfish! Whoa—enough of that tripe. Instead, let's zoom back ahead to right now Tokyo—where I'm nauseous and totally dizzy. From hunger, boredom, disgust, ennui—and probably also major blood loss. Fucko—human pinkies hold a *ton* of blood. Poor Devilfish, your problems are not gorgeous. Let's soothe you with rich deceit. I'd settle for a fried Spam-wich—the raptured stench from a kajillion fast food kiosks was driving me nuts. But even I had enough sense not to rob another fish mart—I'm too easy to pick out. For starters, I'm the wrong shade—the dusky stranger, the jay in a canary flock, a blue 2-ball in a rack of yellow 9s. Plus a bloody hand seems to upset folks. Who veered away from me hissing "Blue Mansu" or "Dumb aloha shirt" or "Hello Gaijan!" Let's have an electrolyte crisis!

Who knows how long I stumbled around in a hematomic haze? I barely remember dirty streets and hick limbs smacking into my dizzy parade. Plus for some odd reason, two dancing bull dogs. Hello Disassociation! It's a bargain between meat and distress—and pain, yeeouch! Now I know what it feels like when I toast humans—eeek, take it away, take it away! I should be dealing death, not feeling it. But ain't this where I get empathetic, rueful, guilty, sobbing with fun regret for eons of nihilistic ease? Dream on, suckers—the only thing I learned was—don't cut off your fingers! Or stick them too far up your nose, ewww. But I def gotta learn to use these new digits—these devious hands are what make you apes lethal. What else could make anthrax and quiche on the same day? Anyway, I finally collapsed on some filthy stairs under a sputtering neon sign for *Prawn Gut Surprise Cafe*. OK, I smell the prawn guts—but where's the surprise? Mine was this beatific face noodling through my delirium. "You're hurt!" it chirped, "wow—you're totally discolored from blood loss."

"Do you like the song 'Urgent'?" I babbled. "*Urgent, so urrrrrrgent—*"

"I'm a doctor—" that chucklehead cooed, "I can *help*."

"Thanks," I moaned, "that's mighty blue of you. Hello Devilfish!"

"Hmmm—shock setting in—no time," and he picked me up—me! Picked up by a biped! And then toted up raw stairs and into a hallway all stanky from kimchee and cats. He was caring for a complete stranger! This clod was dumber than a drunk slug— he even dragged me into a bathroom and slathered me with Bactine and gauze. I'm sure I asked "Is this really your home?" before I bit half his neck off and dropped his dead ass. Hey, he had an apartment— and I needed one! Especially one with cupboards chocked with box-flavored food. At least I didn't eat *him*—or not yet. Instead I gorged on Wheat Thins and stale donuts—both are superb—while inching away from his gushing bod. Ha ha, doctor man— that'll teach you to help weird drifters—Hello Devilfish! We starve in your dumb applause.

Anyway, then I stuffed his gouged neck with a dish towel, plopped him in a closet and watched some TV. It's how us gangstas do our bling thang! We're obviously total morons. But even worse than rerun sitcoms or sadistic game shows—my fave was *Win Prizes or Neuralgia*—all the TV news was about Squidra! My jealousy is buttery hot. Tokyo was *my* playground—mine! Whoa—I gotta figure a way to morph back into a gigantor rapacious Hello Devilfish. And also maybe learn to use these stupid hands— I'd already bought two Datsuns by mistake. How? By banging away on Mr. Dead Doc's laptop—which I found glowing on his kitchen table. How do you work this loony device? Probably *not* by hitting the wrong key with your pinky stump—that just surfed me into a diaper porn site. Wah! Hey, I couldn't use my other hand 'cause it was mostly down my zipper— mmmm. Join us in hot pants languor! Thus spake Hello Devilfish.

ife's full of bees and surprises—with seaweed thrown in for zesty luck! That pretty much sums Tokyo up—surprise, bees, and seaweed—combine them at will. You'll end up with either a failed game show, a new sushi chain or prostitot models slathered with honeycombs. Or a former stingray turned crude human who's banging his pinky stump away on a sticky laptop. Was I researching human growth hormone for clues how to morph back into my proto-ray bod? Scouring med journals for DIY abstracts about how elbows work? Nope—I was just drunk—whee! After guzzling beaucoup sake from that croaked doc's fridge. Look, I'm used to gulping whole rail cars full of rope-a-dope liquor—what, drunk on only nine sakes?

Plus even worse, I was surfing evil, evil Japanese match.com. That snuffed doc had at least twenty fetish hookup pages bookmarked—*Vapid Creampie Housewife* was my fave. Them submissive MILFs made my pants eel point *up*. Hah—there must be some dating lass here who craves a morphed kaiju for her personal household leech. And while sifting through this bevy of fuglies, career Nazis, and absolute loons— no, I would *not* wear a lobster costume at some coastal Kozu trannie weekend—I stumbled across Squidra's profile. Which natch I didn't know was Squidra's yet—Hello Devilfish!

I see much of a kitten here! Really—that was the first line on her bizarre match.com page—*I see much of a kitten*! Hah—right above this crudely photoshopped pic of some thong-clad teen covered with—what are those?—squid tattoos? Along with some bizarre kraken costume accoutrements. Hello Horndog! And goodbye drool that I sprayed laughing—was this profile chick actually wearing rubber calamari socks and tentacle garters? Somehow I'd stumbled across the ultimo Marquis de Cod mate—who else would play at cephalopod sex? Even the Romans weren't that kinky. But mostly I figured her as some art chick with maritime bravado, a Boheme trickster screening out the hapless with provocative lingo—'cause her entire profile was in Manglish! Custom writ for a mark like me. With wordage like *I touched a tiny sawdust* or *Let's have a biology* or *Hello Demon Fish!* Hmmm—where'd I hear *that* phrase before?

Look—any other ray with our normal walnut-sized brain would've caught on it was Squidra! But my stupidity is brave—plus who knew she could type? Though that airbrushed babe's kraken get-up should've set off every *voopa voopa Star Trek* red alert in my numb skull. But I was much intrigued—her fish shtick struck me as pure performance art. And no one bumps uglies like an art girl bent on new euphoria. Even so she kind of overdid it:

> *Me am want meet guy with guyness. Going nude!*
> *Do you pork? We simmer in your bed casserole.*
> *Do me with glad sauce! And you can say to a*
> *man with a job "You are much of a thing." Hello*
> *Demon Fish! Let's be glad with gladly qualities.*
> *I am learning your big language.*

I am much dog aroused! With extra woof sauce. I pictured us in some waterfront bar, her skirt flickering up her nether thighs, her thong shifting into black naptha shadows—happy duping sex machine—Hello Devilfish! Are we tired of me yet? Apparently not as I typed out a reply, cracked open a frosty Sapporo and waited on fate sauce with extra cheese.

Anyway, it was later o'clock when that laptop beeped alive with spanky email. *More Love Than Moose With Squirrel* the subject line said—groovy! It must be that squid-pervy match.com chick. Either that or more spam for Mumbai Viagra made from the freshest battery slag. Acquire our toxic lead boner! Why not—anything's better than another hour of Tokyo TV, a Dada swamp made from rotting crayons and laughing gas. So I muted *Mr. Frog Cripple*—this game show with bizarre tasks like *Please taunt my dead rhino*—and clicked that email. Which was um, mostly cuttlefish porn—even more bizarre pics of red tentacles snaking through rubber camisoles. Are all human bitches this whack? Fine by me—I *like* naxty chicks. Especially sizzling Yakuza molls buttered with wet DNA. All I want is an implausible girl with peachy thighs. She should date me for a husband that has common ideals. Anyway—here's her reply:

> *Hi stranger than a male—Hello Demon Fish! I am a product for a thing you crave. We are meeting like hot dogs and Paris. We are more love than moose with squirrel. We are maids for each other—hubba hubba! Meet me at The Busty Slug, 2 Nippon Quan Drive in an hour? I'm the girl wearing seaweed. Smooches!*

Hmmm—real seaweed or metaphorical? Uh oh—was I dancing down that dank alley where infatuation gets conked on its Easter bonnet and reality rapes your face—meaning was this chick stone nuts? Did she ever drop the *I'm a squid* bit? I'm falling for Squidra's hookup lure 'cause I'm naïve about nooky—how'd she even know I'd find a laptop? Got me—girls are tricky. So natch I emailed her back and we arranged a date. Guys are dependable that way—we're flies checking out webs for the hottest spider. *Help meeeee—oooo baby—brzzzzt.* Plus maybe that café would serve boffo grub—I was mondo famished. Let's plotz with sugar fatigue! Sure, I could snack on that dead Buraku doc—but he was already getting ripe. I even spit out the toes I tried to chow down—ewww. They tasted like feet.

16

Time to hit the love mines! I'm hoping for a girl who loathes my glad career life. Meaning first I'd better re-wrap this oozy pinky stump—thing leaked like a mofo. And then maybe rob that dead doc's wallet—I need cashola for my big pervy date! I have only small bling. Except yucko—his pockets were rigor gooey when I rummaged around for his wallet. "Thanks, um—Doug," I read his ID. Cool— now I'm called Hello Doug! Sweet—I got a fake name, I kill friendlies, I'm psycho drunk—I'm finally a writer, yay! Anyway, then I grabbed shoes and a new shirt—that aloha number was getting truly skanky—and headed down to the subway. Where white-gloved helper guards pack you in closer than gay anchovies—maybe they'll douse us all with spicy soy oil next. Till Squidra grabs the train, yanks some hidden pull tab and dumps us all in her rubbery mouth! Fine by me—crumpling death might cure this horrid rice wine hangover—those nine sakes churned my skull into pufferfish stew. Hello Doug should smooch his body and not be a such drunk—Hello Doug should do lots of stuff. Mwah ha ha—maybe Hello Doug should write a *novel* about stuff.

Your dream empire is without snoozing guests— and you can't cop a hungover nap on these commuter trains neither. Not when you're stacked prick to butt with sixty aftershave-drenched sarary men muttering "Blue Mansu" at you. Nothing like a half hour of breathing knock-off *Old Spice* to make you fond of oxygen. Dunk your tongue in factory juice! I was coal-tar dizzy when I finally stumbled up a platform escalator and into a Hello Delusion street- scape. With pulsing billboards for *Grim Life Tofu* or *Queasy Deodorant*, featuring epileptic visuals and nubile jailbait. What does all this boiled glitter mean? Beats me—give up on sense—embrace the glowing pop goddess as she gilds your neurons with corporate goop. What else you gonna do—read? Let's thrive in happy bliss Japan! And get entranced like me—by that shiny café with a big-eyed Lucite sea slug on top. Whose neon speech balloon said *Busty Slug! Let's Looking For Fun.* I see much of a comedy here as I snort till snot gilds my nose— only the Japanese could meld the preteen sleaze of Hello Kitty with the ickiest sea beast alive. And so ha ha I giggled while my grisly fate throbbed only footsteps away.

My needs are simple—all I want is chaos and steak! And maybe those two chicks in fish costumes hawking slug samples out front—one hottie dressed as a seahorse and the shorter one as a clam, both chanting "Sea slug! Get slug!" at bored commuters. I already pictured them both in my illicit condo, stripping select yummy zones while we writhe in our lust-gummi bed. Hey—how hard can it be to meet a few girls in franchise garb? I gotta do something while I wait on my match.com date—she's very squid obsessed!

Duh—what I should've done was tromp back to Buraku town and avoided large trouble! I have a fun trouble. Anyway, back to my throbbing fate—which ain't all that's throbbing. I was sprouting major wood from watching Seahorse Chick hand out pureed slug samples, her perky tits cupped with green she-beast latex. She must be luscious sweaty in that costume—I got dehydrated just watching her. Either that or from that shrimp-head crepe I scarfed from that dead doc's fridge—you never know. Sure you do—Hello Doug! Lies are fun with mouths. And mouths are fun with pricks—something about that seahorse hottie's rubber tongue twanged every male synapse in my spermy medulla. "Treats from the sea," she passed out more samples, "very slimy!"

"Bargains for the insane!" Clam Girl wiggled her fake shell. Hey—they speak-a the Manglish too! All the hip kids are talking it. "What you got?" I leaned in. "Tits from the sea—very horny treats!" she danced around, "eat my writhing cannibal slop!"

"Nooooo thanks," I winced—who eats sea slugs? They're like crossing boogers with spiders—and this gunk was worse. I give you the Slugwich—puréed frozen soft-serve mollusk swirled on a rice-cake cone. You could even get sea urchin spikes or carp-scale sprinkles on top—your slug needs big flavor! But I *was* starving—I hadn't wolfed anyone down for hours! Us Devilfish are semper-vores—we kill to eat and eat to kill. It's like sex with pancakes and strangers! Wait, sorry—that's just the Manglish jingle some nearby breakfast dive kept playing. *It's happy time with syrup—it's sexing with your pancake!* And speaking of sex syrup, where was my match.com date? She's later than Jesus! And twice worth the wait—in her pics she smoldered like a thermite nightingale. My cock is a lush viper snake!

"Why you tinted so *blue*?" Seahorse Chick grabbed my arm, "from a furby party? From Comic Con?"

"It's a full-body Yakuza tattoo," I smirked. Smirking fun for everyone!

"And what's with your pinky?" she pointed at my bandaged stump.

"You know—bad honor, gangsta boss says cut off my finger," I fibbed about being Yakuza.

"Makes sense," Seahorse Chick shrugged.

"Goop from the ocean," Clam Girl bowed to a German dude, "horribly tasty!"

"Ist gut?" he puzzled.

"Nope!" Clam Girl yelled. Not to worry—he's German. They'll eat anything—pigs, cabbage, history—anything except pureed slugs. "Ewww," that Rhine monkey passed his sample back. "I'll try it," I grabbed his slug muck. Which tasted like hippos smothered with toe gravy—I could barely down it all in one gulp. "Hey," I drooled, "got any more?"

"Blue mansu is *hungry*," Seahorse Chick grinned, "bigger samples inside—follow me!" she shuffled away in full rubber regalia. Mmmm—she smelled like a pile of burnt tires. So natch I tagged along— hey, she had food *and* tits. Pretty much all us dudes need to start into our peacock dance. You know the steps—dance dance, joke joke, plead plead, baby baby, please call 911. When we wake up stabbed or in jail or peering through another smashed eye socket at our hammer-wielding sweetie. Love is your personal brand! Which leads to cooler niche brands like betrayal, lust and murder—and I'm def eager to buy them all. And triple def eager for Seahorse Chick, all sweat lubed in sea latex, her tail doing a gummi-worm hula. I can haz booty? Maybe a happy tete-a-butt in some dark stockroom, our surimi-greased fingers seeking heat and wiggly parts? Mwah ha ha—nope! As fate closed in like an army of frog mummies. Let's be paying grim attention—Hello Doug! All your ADHD are ours.

17

Men—throw off your brains! You have nothing to lose but your balls. I come not to kill the Law, but to complete it—with real laws like cheat the poor. Jail the drifter. Bash the fag. Pimp out your kid. And wear goofy hats, don't forget *that* honker—eeek—even I'm tired of me. And even more tired of all your whiny, weak-assed fiction—been abused? Write a novel. Been a ho, a bum, date-raped by a priest? Write another novel. Till you got libraries crammed with the collective bitching of a jillion victims—who still find time to write! It's enough to discourage even me. But not enough to *stop* me—you need to ride a fish straight to hell! Your extra mild with horseradish hell—mwah ha ha—just try and shut me up. Books are just paperweights thrown to the drowning—especially these nouveau hipster screeds about alien strap-ons and toe-sucking nuns—they're *so* mod. Mod about two centuries ago—Hello Dada! These weekend beatniks just dodge real questions like *Why does that squirrel hate me? Why can't I get laid by Beyonce? Where's all the free pork chops?* I don't even need to crush these ink-maimed wretches—just lurk around their story corners, raising my tail now and then—Hello Devilfish! Let's looking for flaws.

Anyway, then I traipsed after Seahorse Chick into *The Busty Slug*. Where cooks wearing fakey slug antenna caps screamed for more rice and nori. Was this my foodie Promised Land—or just demented franchise girl's house of latex bondage? I wish—that'd be *fun*. Plus fucko McSucko, it was *cold* in here—it takes a mighty Freon blast to freeze slug gristle into soft-serve ooze. But like they say, it ain't the meat, it's the milieu—and this fast-food Antarctica put even Walmart to retail shame. How? With gaudy colors and wailing noise and pure freaky behavior—shivering counter girls twirling slug surimi onto cones, customers frothing nonsense and cash—but what topped it all was the screaming. "He wants a happy treat!" a cook howled. "It's yummy!" the cashier wailed, flipping her cap antenna like rasta dreads. While cooks roared "Busty Slug! Busty Slug!" at hapless customers. Fucko—this dive was a raving deaf fest! "Gimme the grub!" a customer roared. Maybe 'cause of that overhead LCD banner where an anime slug said *Yell Like Me And Get Prizes*! Alright! Only Tokyo could make you order screeching food.

"Have a big treat!" a cook shoved a Slugwich sample in my face. "Sure!" I gulped that squishy mess. "Make him eat more!" the cashier screamed at dancing Seahorse Chick. While shier customers clutched their Slugwich coupons and slunk away, hoping to find a saner franchise. Mwah ha ha—there is no saner franchise. But this Hamburglar inferno seethed with meltdown chaos—my kind of energy— so I might as well stick around. Hey, I gotta do something while I wait on my no-show match.com squid fetish date—her lateness angers me glumly! I'd already planned tipsy dinners where I lick sashimi off that art girl's thighs—or any other foodstuff she hopefully brings with. Uh oh, maybe she smelled my poverty—even wifi can't hide that shizit—and dumped me before we even met.

"Samples!" Seahorse Chick motioned a cashier over. Who wailed "He deserves plenty grub!" and bowed at me. So natch I bowed back—Japanese etiquette pretty much imitates those bobbling drunky-bar bird toys. "Hello Slugwich!" he screamed. "Um, same to you," I whispered, hoping to maybe calm his bonker sonics. Dream on—that entire workforce ramped the decibels up, chanting "Hel-lo Slug-wich!" and banging pots on stainless counters. "It's full of sexy protein!" the cashier squealed. Makes sense— why else would anyone eat frozen slug? It's like chewing a bleach bottle. And no amount of wasabi-infused "spawn sauce" is gonna shield your tongue from that oncoming salt coma. Japan's been on a sodium Jones for millennia—who else makes candy from eel heads? Boil me in hot luck!

But no hot luck for me—'cause they suddenly stopped doling out samples. Why? Um, probably 'cause my date finally showed. I could tell 'cause all the windows burst. In an ear-jangling *keeee-rash*— fucko! What now? Was North Korea finally attacking?

Or was it just another bone-melting earthquake like they get every six hours here? Nope—it was my gooey snookums. Hello Squidra! "Nyah nyah," she stuck her fugly tongue out, "you *fell* for it. My match.com trap!" As her tentacles lashed past the counter, grabbing and twisting Seahorse Chick into a latex croissant. "You stop talking to other ladies," Squidra munched that human pastry, "you only kiss me!" But lips that suck brains out will never suck mine—not with bad breath like a homeless ocean. A writhing pink and sticky ocean—hmmm. Squidra reminded me of *something*—but I couldn't quite pin it. Something damp and furtive on a June evening tinted with beer and raised skirts. But all that raised now was voices chanting *Oooo* while everyone's cell phones taped this smarmy carnage. Hey, it was flash dramatic—as Squidra dropped half-gnawed Seahorse Chick and then eeek, wrapped those Velcro tentacles around my back. "You're a *cute* little changeling," she drooled human rib bits, "come to mama."

"Nope—Hello Stabby!" I grabbed some chopsticks and lanced at her gummy suckers. "Hee hee—tickle me Demon Fish!" Squidra snorted, drizzling murder goo all over everyone. Whoa—learn to cover your mouth! Or beak or whatever that thing is. While her tentacles whirred like a flesh propeller, knocking customers and stunned cooks into walls or stoves or whatever other cheap decor got in her way. Let's have a décor—Hello Doug! Hah—Hello Doug should maybe escape now and not talk so cute. Hello Doug's a moron—I just gawked and oozed fear funk while Squidra churned everyone into death sludge. "Come on, baby," she hissed, "let's work on our *feelings*." Great—it's always helpful and delicious when life turns into cartoons. And feet into panic when I skedaddled out of that collapsing slug shack, giggling like a baby hyena. 'Cause hey, Squidra's match.com profile didn't lie—she *was* wearing a ton of seaweed.

'm a reality snack—Hello Devilfish! Let's not again. Not what—commit mayhem, murder, tedium? Let's start with murder—it's chaos on a stick! And what drives this junked Volvo of a universe—join our tasty shoa! Hey, assembly-line death *is* pretty cool. But even murder gets boring—death's just a cosmic plumber, a butt-crack slob phoned in to clean out the clogged pipes. Worshipping a vulture god like that's a total waste of jizz. The trick is to have lethal *fun*—to put the *yow* back in Dachau. When I first set out to destroy Big Lit I thought your taboos actually mattered. *Just violate a few of these hummers,* silly me thought, *and their mental empire will collapse.* I was ready to whore out tweeners, smear babies into beige butter, scream racist epithets till I turned even bluer—till I found out it simply *entertains* you. You like hearing nuts rave—why else read *me*?

Someone tortured you, maimed your kid, mushed your hubby into war grease? Don't write about it— kill them. Slay them in their beds and McMansions, their boardrooms and yachts—hunt them down for sport, wear an Elmer Fudd hat while you unload your wabbit gun into their spraying necks, smear boot-black on your cheeks and sneak with ninja grace into their granite kitchens, driving a Ginsu knife through their smarmy hearts—do something besides type it up! Words are fangless kittens—Hello Devilfish! Really—you're wracked with love and itches? You pine for impossible Betty? Then buy her some daisies and take her to Funkytown—just stop scribbling about it!

Anyway, then I crawled over dead *Busty Slug* Squidra victims—let's evade with much torpor! 'Cause I still ain't learned to walk good, mostly stumbling crab-wise down streets gooey with squished limbs and squashed clam-nectar kiosks. Ms. Tentacle Butt's def on the chaotic rag. So bathtub with me while I trip over another twitching corpse—Squidra's eyeball lasers sometimes make them flop all galvanic red for hours—and let's search for rude shelter. Which got really rude when some gangstas shoved me out of their basement stairwell, screaming *Get bit* in Yakuza slang. Join our happy scapegoat club! 'Cause I'll def get much blamed if anyone finds out Squidra's only after *me*—that I'm the rube ex-ray what triggered her big pink estrus. Her hanky-panky is extra abundant!

Hello Carnage! And bloodshed and guts as I bobbled through the Financial Prefecture, pixel ads for *Gitmo Sweat* sports drink sizzling on cracked billboards while skyscrapers snapped and oozed human marrow—whoa! Somehow it all reminded me of Bible class. Eeek—it is God-ra! Crushing Tokyo with his jumbo gold sandals. And what does that stalker cephalopod think I'll give her, anyway? Maybe snuggly intimacy with me nodding off while she drones on about how her goddamn punk brother burnt her favorite Barbie—Hello Spouse! So trick your brain with sense again while I stand and hyperventilate. 'Cause shhh—I just heard this horrid gloopy noise like jihad snot. Eeek, it's my rubbery cuttlefish date! Who's smashing stores and buses, sniffing the debris for my biped scent. No. 1 Towel Production OK!

So pet your fury harder while I scramble away. Hah—we learned that much from 9/11—don't wait around for the second jet. And get out of the way, fucknuts! Meaning these sarary hordes strolling past me, clutching laptops and delusions. They're way too blasé about that nearby slimy kaiju squid churning Tokyo into concrete sorbet—apparently nearby ain't near enough. It's like at that pinky-chopping fish mart—if Mothra ain't right on your ass, why worry? Ask any Israeli—no imams lurking on the loading dock? Then no terror sick-day for *you*. Or me as I swayed quicker through seething streets—you gotta run from smoochy love. Especially from a hormone-tweaked squid bending trucks and roads to her wobbly will. "Darling—we need to *talk*—" she coos, mashing cars and streetlamps into steel granola, "you owe me that much—you *promised*." Huh? When did I promise her anything except hate and disdain?

Lucky for me Squidra lost my scent, turning her fluttering bulk toward the sea—probably heading back to some weird Sponge Bob coral hut with a whale skull foyer. I was safe for now—another superb mammal motto. Safe for now! Join our stupid coward club—all you need is terror and feet. Too bad about dead Seahorse Chick—she smelled panic luscious in her sweaty rubber negligee—but I'd already boned her in my mind. Which is where most human boning takes place anyway—for sex-crazed bonobos, you guys hardly get *any*. And I'm getting less! Pity my lonely, lonely dong—it should be copping drunk titty sex with stripper chicks! These anthro wangs are somewhat demanding—my lust is a thing for big censure. And so are demented Squidra's dude-on-squid fantasies— she's more twisted than a licorice tornado.

Anyway, I wobbled through night Tokyo till I ended smack back in that Buraku district. Why am I drawn to bum life? Probably the fish and death stench—it smells like stingray home. And then I saw a green rooster. Not an actual rooster—that clucker wouldn't last a famished minute in broke Buraku-town. Nope, this fowl was super-sized—meaning that girl in a bantam costume shedding feathers near a furby bar. Whoa—a fur-real furby bar! Listen, a Tokyo furby bar is not to be missed or dissed. 'Cause unlike

American furries—those chubby pervs who wear rent-a-mammal costumes for a night of dry-humping cartoon booty—Tokyo furbies put the hot back in haute. Plus a furby bar means cosplay—that's costume-play in J-Pop speak. I'd read websites about cosplay orgies in ruined warehouses. Mmmm, sounds delish—a yelping pile of anime girls in manimal garb, a farm-fest fuck mosh crammed with warbling human tail. Hello Devilfish! I'm as delirious as a boiled preemie.

Was I invited? Should I sneak in? Hah—anywhere's better than waiting around for stanky Squidra. Plus maybe I'll get laid here! Either that or snookered into a Badz Maru Tupperware party—you never know with these fur-dom freaks. As testosterone sugars surged through my veins while slit twats danced on my mind. I'm doing the hormone polka! No wonder I'm totally doomed—Hello Devilfish! I touched a tiny doom. And was def ready to touch pretty much anyone—my peepee's a sad bachelor. Not for long—the sidewalk outside this furby bar was chocked with fashion slatterns, Ganguro hotties in superfly fly suits, Yamanba blackface babes, and barely-legal morsels dressed up as Bo Peep or her bendable lamb. Just like at *The Busty Slug*—Tokyo's cuckoo for costumes. Japan's pretty much a permanent Halloween.

A Halloween with cooze and booze—alright—time to hustle! My lobster-hot Jimmy craves wet-time fun. But hmmm, without sufficient bling—how to get in? That dead doc's wallet was pretty cash poor. And I doubt my usual *Us morphed stingrays don't carry much yen* scam would work here. Ahhh, goofy Japan—I must count on my blue gaijan exoticness—all I gotta do is lurk around. Sure enough, I get tapped on the shoulder by Rooster Girl. "Blue mansu—we are having a social time!" she slaps me with her fake wing. Everything's fake—get used to it. "And BTW," she touches my bare arm, "nice Smurf costume."

"What costume?" I act dumb. It's not as hard as you think—think harder!

"Whoa—cool skin," she pinches me, ow, "how'd you dye it?"

"It's a dumb story," I grit my teeth. What—now I gotta narrate stuff?

"Grab your bongos, Mr. Blue Mansu—let's have a fuck party!" she giggles.

"Sounds groovy," I nod. Except uh oh—I am in a dicey neighborhood—what if she's Buraku? How could I endure the shame? First I'll need to learn what shame even is. "I know the doorman—free entry! You got money for drinks?" Rooster Girl squints way too close at my pockets—these Tokyo chicks ain't shy about wallet inspection. I see much of a doomsday here! Better make shit up. "Blue Mansu knows the bartender," I fib. My art, you are my art. Let's never make sense. "I'm a chicken!" Rooster Girl pats her clammy fowl costume, "a really damp chicken." True dat—her bare knees were sweating worse than mayo at a marathon. I can haz picnic sex? As we slide into that manimal bar and hopefully her libido's waiting room. "Brak buk buk," Rooster Girl crows, "I'm a big hen!" No worries—how many tragedies start with that line?

19

O Japan, you have mouths and pantsuits—let's never disagree. Except about how god-awful hideous Tokyo pop is—the stuff sounds like fried mynahs. Hello Cacophony! As a furby party doorman bowed us into a room sick with sluggish light. Whoa—it was animal havoc inside—anime critters, manga mascots, duck and pig and peacock manimals all glugging cheap sake and prancing around like Satan's lice. Uh oh—cheap sake can lead to no good. Especially since I already downed two cups. Imagine mixing peyote, Nazi pee, and devil snot—and then throwing that away and glugging cheap sake. That shit was brain Drano. My drift is powerful and hopeful! My lips were already numb. But I gotta admit—I was in prime form. When I somehow convinced myself Squidra could never find me here—happy delusion—Hello Idiot! I see much of a numbnuts.

And much of a poontang too! Yee haw—this furby hump-a-thon was just the squid-ducking cover I needed. I could blend in—my blue skin has much costume advantage. Plus I was maybe guaranteed some hot beast sex—either with Rooster Girl or any other fine drunk she-manimal. Dressing up for anonymous sex is always a hit in repressed cultures—ask any mascot. Let's boink like slugs, slow and delicious. But hmmm—with who? That girl dressed as a samurai fox? Mwah ha ha—maybe she wore a six-nipple bra underneath. I liked her hick vixen dancing style—Hello Orgy! 'Cause everyone here seemed def ready to naxty—a lush Sargasso Sea of manimal butts wiggling in a slo-mo frenzy. Join us in pants snarfling fun! "Just watching, huh?" Rooster Girl grabbed someone else's sake and glugged that slop down, "OK then. Let's watch." She is much a zesty mouthful!

"Hello Blue Mansu!" some octopus chick in a cheap tiara tugged my shirt, "let's groove!"

"Cool," I wiped drool and memory off my lips. My biceps are pabulum strong! Meaning not strong enough to keep Rooster Girl nearby. Nope—some wandering dragonfly dude already snatched her, both giggling and dripping spilled booze as they booked somewhere hidden—with octopus chick tagging along! Let's feel bad and some lonely. Hello Doug needs a better mating sense—hah—that and more rotting rice wine. At least there's no Squidras here— that gooey kraken's got cuddly-wuddly plans. Don't she know I'm too tiny for her humongous twat? Love is a jealous stuff—get it away! 'Cause all I craved now was chicken booty, to slam against Rooster Girl and gnaw her ratty wings till she blossomed nude from sweaty feathers. It would be cool if she sucked my tool, too. My heart primps for nooky—with a brave and sugar passion!

And you can't fool a waking dick. Hmmm—maybe I could join that seething biped pile over there—but they looked like mostly dudes. And no way I'm sucking any Johnsons tonight—let's not have the gay. Or not till I got smashed enough—hah—liquor has sexy ideas. And sake's remarkably crabby—like that drunk raccoon girl slapping her date with psycho paws. Got me why—you never know what's gonna set these mofos off. And just as quick it was over—someone said the magic Japanese word about seppuku or ancestors or shame—Hello Devilfish! Then I guzzled more sake till my pants eel rose like a drunk moon—gimme some rampant cooze! Let's have the fuck life. As Rooster Girl stumbled back, grabbed me and then stuff happened with taxis and stairs. Evil, lurching stairs—I was too wasted to tell up from now or left from later. Who cares about sequences anyway? Realism is like bad acting—you get bored and want popcorn. I spit on realism and all its cunning henchmen!

20

Hey kids—use your crayons to help Mr. Devilfish escape from his placemat maze! Save the red one for his dingus. I'm def trapped—in a plot backwater ripe with croaking prose and pulp sludge. What clod god made this karmic swamp? Where us poor stingrays swipe at chuckling fireflies while the Big Dipper ladles us with doom syrup? Beats me—afterlife questions are best left to your oppressors. But I gotta regain my blue mojo—no rest for the vapid! I'll screech *geeraa* and raise on my wings—sorry, arms, whatever—and crush someone—anyone—to snuff this boredom. Mwah ha ha—boredom's the best killer, nothing beats it. *It was a balmy day filled with storks and ennui. Elmer, my half cousin on my mom's dad's uncle's side—they all had lupus or strawberry leprosy—stroked his iPad and mused about kale.* Hello *Paris Review*!

I know—I'll morph myself into a Xbox game. *Hello Devilfish—The Final Quorum.* It'll be FPS—first person shooter—with my flaming spit and toxic tail as your weapons. Be sure to reload that fire widget before your napalm runs out! Don't like that boss, that girl-friend, that boy toy, that job? Blast away, mofos—ignore the cheesy graphics, the CGI puppies, and Shriners dead in a billion trenches. *It had to happen, there were forces at work*—hah! You fuckers kid your killers and kill your kids—you bipeds will snuff your-selves plenty without me. I'm just the cosmic garnish, the ticking cherry some nightshade hand gently plops on your holocaust sundae. Let's have a gory dessert! For all your martial needs. Look, all I ever wanted was—everything! The world shivering in my wing—hand, whatever—drizzled with mint auroras and baked to a starry crisp. With lots of screams and thick penis fun! I craved murder and pussy and hot stingray sprees, hawking flame loogies through filthy rain while you nudniks shriek and aim drooping har-poons—Hello Freud! All your id are ours.

Anyway, then night was either blue or dark. The wind and my mind moved as one. Right—except I wasn't banging cheap shutters around. Let's hide your secret hairs! 'Cause the long black ones on that pillow def weren't mine—or those polystyrene feathers neither. Fucko—what rabid manimal pup did I take home last night? Oh, right—that chicken girl. *Mwah ha ha* I chuckled as flotsam post-party scenes bobbled through my mind—me puking in a cab and the driver screaming ideograms—me falling up apartment stairs one bruised knee at a time—me snoring while Rooster Girl slapped my limp dick around—with lots of blackout amnesia marbled through this memory meat. Meaning I probably didn't bone her—drunky wiener-slap rarely leads to a stiffy—but what else maybe happened? My head is sleek with booze puzzles! I'm a snooze cocktail brewed from crispy alcohol thirst—let's blame sake for my flaws! Let's have a blame. My brain felt soggier than shark spit—Hello Doug has much ethanol trauma.

And also amazingly crusty gums. So brush your teeth with *Biopaste*! It has chemicals for your longing. Hey, at least the stuff tastes minty—you never know with Japanese dental products. Believe me—do *not* try *Tsunami Breath Mouthwash.* Anyway, so I'm scrubbing last night's tempura off my molars—Rooster Girl made me learn me that hygiene trick—when I heard something gloop closer. "What the—" I leaned through her tiny bathroom window—a cricket couldn't see dick through this dwarf hole—but all I heard was crickets. That and my own wheezy breathing—these monkey lungs work like wet concertinas.

But a life of booze, murder, and hot furby booty ain't bad—maybe I could get used to staying human. As long as I never get a job—hah—you bipeds are slave donkeys. Any boss with a whip and a slogan can keep you suckas toiling. Maybe if I tricked Rooster Girl with love I could sponge off her—Hello Metrosexual! All your spike mousse are ours. Still— what's with that glooping noise? No way Squidra could find me here—this ain't even my apartment. For sure not—the place was freezing—brrr! How do you bipeds stay warm? Duh, with clothing—so I donned this kimono I found on the floor—some fuchsia number dotted with cartoon carrots. WTF?

Was it designed for chicks or dudes? But instead of fashion delirium, maybe I should've watched those chintz bedroom curtains. Where eight sneaky stealth tentacles flexed at the moon—Hello Calamari!

Here's a story with girls and squids. OK—it was almost dawn out. Birds screamed about bugs. Cars wandered around like Alzheimer's patients. Plus whoa—I needed some breakfast—I hoped Rooster Girl had some grub in her dinky fridge. But uh oh—maybe she'll wake up and want smooches. Eeek! So far I'd gotten off easy—no violence, no weeping, no promises I couldn't fudge my way out of—maybe nooky in Japan actually *was* guilt-free. Hah—dream the fuck on. Nooky's always barbed with hell bait—evolution's just one long demonic infomercial. And where was Rooster Girl anyway? Did she ditch both me and her own apartment? Cool—I could use a new pad. 'Cause by now that Buraku doc's corpse stank up his condo into a cop-luring stench. Hello Maggots! It's best to avoid the moist dead.

"Want some coffee? Rooster Girl yelled from her kitchen. "Mmmm—java," I wandered in where aha—Rooster Girl ain't no chicken no more.

Nope—she was radiant naked, a skin sylph whispering dawn off each florid curve—Hello Meat Treat! I got a major chub just gawking at her—human weenies are *quick*. "Do you take cream?" she tilted her hip. "Anytime," I reached at her damp cooze. "Wait a sec," she leaned away, "what's that noise?"

"I dunno," I shrugged, "maybe giant krakens are sneaking through your windows." And that's when I heard those slurpy cheeps only squid suckers make. "Do you hear something *liquid*?" Rooster Girl frowned as eeek, morbid tentacles crashed through her kitchen blinds! Till a few wrapped round my shoulders and I smelled that hobo ocean scent—Hello Squidra! How'd she find us? She has wholesome tracking skills. "Nice kimono," she gurgled squid snot.

"Um—thanks," I edged away.

"Why the boner, Mr. Demon Fish? Let me smell you," she snarfled closer, "whoa—are you *fucking* this bitch?" Ahhh, mind your own beeswax. And your breath too—that cephalopod needs apocalypse-strength Listerine. "You said you'd be *faithful*," Squidra poked her beak through that smashed window. Huh? Faithful to what—idiocy? Love me, dump me, eat me, date me, tempt me, shoot me, hump me, leave me—yow! At least she has goals. Baste me in girl juice!

Let's be modest with modest qualities. And get back to that yummy carnage where Squidra lashes even more tentacles through mashed glass and squeezes Rooster Girl! "Honor your commitment," Squidra brays, "or the slut gets it!" and I both cower and shrug. While Rooster Girl puddles into organ fluids near a toaster—and what? I'm supposed to save her? It ain't like we're friends—all we did was hump. "Your choice—" Squidra screams, "love me—or mayhem!" and stinks up the place with her bottom-fish breath. Plus *fucko* is she ugly—that head like a gummy vibrator, that eye like a gangrened planet, those pulsing suckers that long to smother me with damp affection. Plus what's she wearing—a polka-dot skirt? Some awning no doubt ripped from a theater marquee—which did *nothing* for her hips. "Stop undressing me with your eyes," Squidra snarls, "use your hands!"

"OK," I swing a nearby IKEA lamp at her beak— which she simply gnaws to twinkly bits. Grrr,

grrr—now I can't even snuff one measly squid? Come on—killing stuff is why I attacked Tokyo! Hah—instead I'm the mark in the looniest grift of all time—the old gigantor-stingray-turned-puny-human bait and switch. At least I've been duped by the best—God is the ultimate carny.

appy Easter with goat sauce! But I had more to worry about than hairy kids right now—like that vicious squid slamming around the kitchen. "We could make whoopee," Squidra coos in my ear, yucko, "and start all over again." This kraken is horny for man meat. Her exerting kisses must win a fresh bed. "Open up to *love*," Squidra lifts her skirt and spreads somewhere pink—eeek! Is love always that stanky? "How about some coffee first?" I smash a fresh carafe full into her face. Till she collapses in a cuttle-fish heap screeching "Hot! Hot!" and spurting frantic ink. Hello Devilfish! I'm amazed I'm still alive. Unlike thrashing Rooster Girl near the oven, her cracked belly leaking poop-sausage loops. "Oooo—candy," Squidra cracks that girl's skull like a glass bonbon.

"Whoa," I gawk, "did you just kill my date?"

"She was your *date*?" Squidra grins like jealous dentures. Do squid even *have* teeth? "Ewww," Squidra plucks snack hair off her beak, "messy little bitch."

"Great," I sidestep twitching Rooster Girl chunks, "*now* who's gonna clean up?"

"Not us, baby," Squidra slithers closer, "and take that kimono *off*."

"No!" I wrap myself tighter, "you're letting a draft in! I'm *cold*. And who made *you* boss?"

"I will rule your soul," Squidra winks.

"Booty macht frei," I snarl back. Sorry, I know— Nazi jokes are *so* twentieth century. But I gotta troll for the easy borscht-belt laughs—noshing squids are a tough crowd. Hello Chutzpah! Yep, the fun never stops here—it just stops being fun. Well, when in Rome do as the Visigoths did—smash stuff and rape nuns—so I grab a chair and make ready to go all Captain Nemo on this kraken's ass. Who just gulps that chair and then smooths her polka-dot skirt. I was right—it *is* a marquee tarp. It's easy to see now 'cause that kitchen wall's long gone. "Just me—no other girl-friends!" Squidra roars. What gives with this cuttlefish? She's a product I can't agree on—let's submission with me! "You *know* my heart beats for you," Squidra coos, spraying ink loogies in my face, "why you so cruel?" Hah—Squidra was digging for guilt, tapping into that male shame vein chicks mine out daily. Picture them toting IUD pickaxes and toiling away in ovarian shafts, singing Seven Dwarves songs and wiping spermicide froth off their brows. Never leave a guy alone with an idea. Never tell us the truth either—we're not programmed to deal. So put a smile with your lips and fib along with me! "Um sure—I got *big* love," I shiver as tentacles wrap my legs, "heap big love only for *you*—Rooster Girl meant *nothing* to me." That part's actually true.

"Prove it," Squidra sulks, "come to counseling with me."

"Huh? What?"

"I found a raptor in Osaka that does couples counseling. We could learn to *communicate*—"

"Yeah, um, undoubtedly baby," I purr, "great idea. I'll call *you*. Just write your phone number on the wall with some blood," I check around for exits. "No!" Squidra rears like an enraged pink Slinky, "no more *ditching* me. Give it *up*," she slithers suckers around my butt, "gimme your man rod." Squidra's def a classic weird stalker chick—she needs lessons in booty etiquette for her very mating needs.

"*Bay-ay-ay-by—let's get together*—" Squidra croons an Al Green tune—with horrid antediluvian warbling dredged from the spanky sea depths. Her tongue is deaf fun! As she munches some last Rooster Girl morsels while flapping her gills at my neck. "*Loving you forevvvvvvvvvver—is all I wanna doooooooo,*" she gurgles like lip pudding. Except pudding knows when to shut up! "Let me at least stroke your weenie," she shakes me like a bottle of shy ketchup. It's shy 'cause it can't leave the bottle—it has very tomato ideals. "Honey muffin," Squidra rattles me harder, "was that a *yes*?"

"Muh-muh maybe www-we should see other pppp-people," I giggle.

"Maybe we should *eat* other people," she puts me down—and then lunges her beak at my head! Luckily I dodge good and she just crushes the fridge into freon pulp. "Alright! Whatever!" I yell, "like I said, write your phone number down and—"

"I need smooches *now*," Squidra rasps like an asp.

"Um, maybe later," I point at Rooster Girl muck, "first I gotta tidy up, and—"

"Now is *always* better, darling," she presses gunky squid flab against me.

"No! Not now," I stomp my teensy foot, "later!"

"No snuggle for Squidra?" Ewww, she gives me that hangdog puppy look—if puppies were ninety feet tall and chewed hippos for breakfast. "OK, Mr. Demon Fish—I gave you a chance."

"You gave me a headache," I laugh.

"And now have big death," she lashes her every runny sucker at me. "Nuh uh," I somehow twist free and scrabble hands at smeary walls, gulping dust and panic. "Love Squidra!" she waves her tentacles like zombie cobras. I'm cute when I digress. As Squidra smacks the whole condo apart, walls shuddering into stucco crud where I smash like a comet through spattering glass.

22

Anyway, then I ducked and wobbled through a rebar goulash set to Squidra Muzak—mostly *Smooch me* gurgles and Dolby grunts. Join our grim soiree! That's pretty much all Tokyo was now—a smoldering hell deli chocked with crushed spleen pâté and torn-butt cold cuts. Whoa! Girlfriend has been *busy*—shhh, hear that murky screech? My kraken sweetie doth waddle hither, stomping thick tentacles through leaky streets, smooshing trucks and mopeds into iron gazpacho. Now wait for it—here they come—her scorching orange laser eyeball rays, yay! That's how she flushes any hid idiots from the wreckage until *Aeeeeee* they're charred to crude carbon. Alright! Who doesn't want a snookums like her?

Me for starters—she ain't my type! No dingbats. But I was def her dreamy fish-man fantasy—maybe she dug my moral torpor. Let's have the confused lifestyle—it's called Moron Life. Does Squidra wants to date, bone, or devour me? No doubt all three—hey, she's a chick—meaning pink, wet, and schizo. I can haz archetype? Still, no reason to make it any easier for that damp beast—there's gotta be some way to elude her radar hearing, suckery arms and dog-squishing bod. Should I maybe go to the cops? Hah—good luck finding any in this steamy rubble. Plus they'd no doubt just lock *me* up for my kimono fashion faux pas—and no way I'm gonna dawdle in some Fuchu dungeon till my pink sweetie shows. *Yes officer—that's him, Mr. Human Demon Fish. He's my Korean love slave! No, keep the gag on—the little fucker bites.* Screw that—my latest hot plan was to board the nearest jet to any-where—we are flying your skies with moxie! And probably crashing on your tarmac—I'd never ditch Squidra that easy. She'd just grab my jet midflight and use it for a toothpick—Hello Revulsion! Let's much avoid her.

And you will say to a morphed stingray—well, how's that gonna happen? All your question are ours—Hello Devilfish! If I say that enough I'll be safe. Safe from what? Safe from pink doom harpies with ribbon-candy teeth—that Squidra wants to kill me *good*. The weird booty memes were probably just thrown in to spice things up. Exactly—it ain't enough that a mad kraken wants to rip me limb from skin— she wants to be *loved*.

But I got smaller things to fret about—like picking smashed kitchen slivers out of my neck, ow. Plus there's big wildfire spreading from that wrecked condo's gas main—get away Hello Doug! Except hmmm, maybe I'm being a mite hasty—how often do talking squids get a crush on you? Opportunity was knocking and I'm always home. Usually drunk on the couch, raving about wetbacks, but still—maybe I could make some bling off this squirrelly cuttlefish! I'll turn her sloppy lust into boffo profit—with a Hello Squidra ad campaign! I pictured juicy sitcom offers, Happy Meal spin-offs, Manglish energy drink endorsements—*Try Tentacle Cola! It's better drinking than Balls Milk*. I could manage her like Colonel Sanders did Elvis—get her hooked on butter and Maalox, then work her to death and cash in.

Should I employ Squidra much? Don't be Hello Doug stupid! And don't hesitate neither, bro—let's join that squid-panicked mob swarming out of Nagano prefecture. Just follow the bouncing limbs! So have some menthol refreshment, tell your pals howdy and crowd along. Where I'm def now surrounded by crazed Buraku masses, broke Tokyo-ites whose social ladder rung is on the paint-splattered bottom. What's the untouchable rush? They'll never escape—the Army already blocked every exit with barbwire and shame, hoping Squidra will eat these clucks first— and maybe get fatal colitis from their sub-caste bods. Nope, their untermensch job is to just hopelessly mill around, clutching pots and toy penguins—which melt into avian soup as Squidra ramps up her melty vision—she's lit with orange rage! As more clueless fighter jets scream down—and then poof into diode dust when her eye lasers zap them. It's gonna be awhile till they figure out how to snuff her wet rump. Ahhh, my murderous ogling sneaky-pie Squidra— she's got a mind brewed from angst and loose teeth.

She's a job with stale honor! And my job is just to stay alive—and evade those gummy streets where Squidra cracks whole apartment blocks open, snarfling the carnage and gurgling "Here, leetle fish man—" Please escape her with me! And limit your yawns again 'cause fucko—what if this mob finds out I'm Squidra's sole goal? No doubt they'll tie me to a plank, dunk me in sherbet and offer Squidra a Hello Doug creamsicle.

Anyway—after body-surfing a clump of floundering cripples, I somehow managed to claw into a subway and board the airport express. I'm so cute—I don't know that Squidra is Armageddon yet! Meaning that prole zone we zip through that's smeared with weepy biomass—have some lymph jello! I can't even ditch her image—Squidra's B-flick pics are *everywhere*—on overhead TVs, iPads, and cheap Laotian Kindles—she's more popular than candied carp fins. Hey, her doom specs are FX groovy—as walls writhe into death spaghetti when her dread tentacles raze another skyscraper that's tall like a thing.

I always think of your thing. Especially when our train zooms through scrawny forests and toward

Narita airport. I am a proud fashion god! Except nobody even notices that foofy carrot kimono I still got on—they're all gossiping about noxious Squidra! She's famous like a place. Grrr, grrr—it should be my Devilfishy fame, mine! And then—like nooky, war, or paychecks—that train simply stopped. With a gnashing *screeeeee* like from sabertooth rats as *duhn duhn duhhhhh*—squid lips gnawed through the car floor. Hello Predator! Hah—it's more fun than Commie panties as Squidra wads train seats into steel origami, sniffing any trapped human pretzels for my scent. "Give him up!" she rakes lasery eyebeams over commuters till they burst into bone popcorn. Squidra's having trouble meeting a boy and she's awkward. And pretty hungry too as she gulps anything drippy. Is that a kidney or a Chihuahua? Ewww—chew with your mouth closed.

23

Number One mind destruction OK! Exactly—time to ditch this dopey culture seething with Manglish, preteen morals, and horny krakens. Mwah ha ha—I'm doomed 'cause I can't escape. Mmmm, escape—ain't that the loveliest human word? And the oldest—you warbled it crawling from sizzling jellyfish oceans onto gasping land—you whispered it stumbling through herds of vampire tigers—you sang it in schuls and trenches and cluster-bombed malls. And all I needed was maybe ten safe minutes to skulk away and make you guys proud. On to the airport! Let's lose our lives.

Hello Woozy Doug! That's me as I crawl from that creamed train and hop across squirming rails. That melt like my luck when Squidra amps up her eye lasers. "Where *is* he?" she thrashes at sprawled commuters, shaking some even deader and then gulping them down. While meanwhile anyone alive seethes away in fear waves, hoping they'll never be next. So why's it always *my* turn? I can't catch a break—or a taxi! Maybe I should just race around in circles like the rest of these human cyclones. And then yummy, I sniffed holy jet fuel spritzing like angel farts. Which meant the Narita terminal's nearby! So let's dodge through a jammed freeway, beep beep crash, then stumble onto—yes! Runway tarmac!

Thank you gone Jesus! Plus I still had that dead doc's ID—I could storm any plane and zoom into the swallowing skies. I figured with all this grim slaughter they won't be too picky about tickets. Then I'll buckle in and slurp Chex Mix and rip-off booze till we level out at ninety thousand feet—somewhere where there ain't flying squids. Till we hopefully jet toward survivalist Utah and some bleak Salt Lake desert—where I'll rent a ruined trailer and find work as a spud wrassler. You gotta have a dream—mine was rattlesnakes, chubby MILFs, and poor cable reception. And also heat, scorching heat—let's have a boiled lifestyle! The hotter the better—even stalker squids can't survive 120 degrees of blazing shade.

Believe me? Why not? 'Cause somehow I actually did board a plane, this midsize prop job where a stewardess grappled me up the gangplank—Hello Rescue! "Sit *down*, blue mansu," she shoved me in a seat that already stank from pee—mostly mine! Do you bipeds always leak when you're scared? I'm sad and can't fathom why I'll never be safe. Especially when something pink this way comes—eeek! It is much Squidra! As that smooch-crazed kraken schleps across tarmac, wraps her sticky tentacles around the nearest 747 and rips it in two, shaking victims like Pixy Stix granules into her chewing mouth. Yucko—you can even see colons drizzling down her sticky flanks. She's a furor I can believe in—Hello Devilfish!

Never use fate as your caterer. As our mad captain throttles us past Squidra, hoping to dodge her spread tentacles—and no such luck. She's on a *love* hunt— puny constraints like physics and entropic mass won't stop her. "Where's my blue mansu?" she shrieks, latching onto our plane and ripping it into tin

shards—with limbs and extra gut sauce! A stewardess
even thinks fast and pops an escape slide open. Till
someone's wallet tumbles down that slide—and some
mope scrambles after it. What's he gonna do—show
death his Walmart card? Too late—Squidra's already
smooshed him and that slide with her pink rump.
She's like a cartoon, only different. "Where's my
leetle love bucket?" she growls, her beady eyeballs
glaring around.

Our happiness is your squalor! But enough elo-
quence—time to get *out*. As passengers leap up and
bonk their vaudeville heads together—and I'm
trapped, wah! No prob—I just swim that yelping
horde like it's an avalanche, frog-stroking over their
punching fists till I flop onto tarmac—mwah ha ha!
Let's have a plot to sneer with. I even ran before I
actually knew how, plopping one dazed foot over
the next like some trepanned lab rat, my brain
pulsing with maze graphics, my hair streaming like
neural implants. Join us in cowering fun! As Squidra
rises in dank majesty, sniffing and gulping huddled
bods and narrowing her gooey gaze. Uh oh—did
she spot me yet? Probably—she's clomping very

closer! But where to escape now—that twisted baggage ramp? That imploding terminal? That raging fuel dump? And then I smacked, ow, smack into an airport bar.

ourage is the bitter part of valor. Good thing I got neither as I sprint into that handy tavern— maybe I can hide in a beer keg, get wasted, and ignore my flailing heart. It's flailing with big hot sugar death magic—Hello Devilfish! Even I can't make this stuff up. But all this dumb terror almost makes me pity you biped suckers—you're scared of everything! Damn straight—it *is* all out to get you. And me too— even that swaying *Hello Drunky Pilot* bar sign that clips my hurt pinky stump, ow, as I enter that dark Yakuza lair. "What's up, doc?" the doorman laughs.

"Huh?"

"The carrots," he taps my veggie-deco kimono. Hey, at least I ain't underdressed—this dive swarms with natty gangstas. Makes sense—Narita's a major hub for drug shipments. I can haz meth? Luckily no murderous minds fixated on me—why would they? If these killers can ignore a rampaging kraken, what's a barefoot dude in ratty silk matter? Which gets even rattier when a nearby bar wall crashes down. 'Cause eeek—it is Squidra! In all her fashionista splendor. Meaning she's wearing a bridal gown stitched together from tarps and sails—where'd she find the time? And the tarps? "Sweetums—ask me to *marry* you," Squidra gurgles, "and let love win."

"Love is a fucktard's game," I giggle and duck a keg Squidra throws. "Hey, you two—" a gangsta cocks his thumb, "take it outside." Screw that—I need to make large romance decisions. Fucko—was Squidra maybe right? Should I pop the question? Trade my big fuck fun bachelor pizazz life for a daily slog of brute work, poopy spawn, and dank loathing? Nah—better to stumble around like a spaz halibut. As Squidra slaps Yakuza out of her way, spritzing gore on the bar mirror. Let's not believe me a bit. "Do it, Mr. Man—propose!" Squidra raves till "Banzai!" a sword-wielding Yakuza attacks her—and chops off a tentacle! Which flops around like a demonic tapeworm while Squidra smacks that Yakuza into bio goo. Watch out, snookums—'cause *duhn duhn duhhhhh*—here come even more samurai gangstas! With seppuku swords they somehow pulled out of their butts—till I hear their necks snapping like soft twigs. Sorry, boys, it's a thankless battle—Squidra pretty much just mops the floor with everyone's guts. Except mine as I crack a cue stick in two and feebly slash at her. "*Stop* that," Squidra giggles, "it *tickles*."

"Enough!" I finally just stand there, courage stirring my brain into a war martini, "what do you *want*?"

"Some attention would be nice," Squidra mopes, "a poem now and then. Some passion. Maybe a few kids."

"And how's *that* gonna happen?" I toss that broken cue, "ain't you noticed? A slight difference in our sizes?"

"Nooky conquers all—mmmm," Squidra gnaws on fresh Yakuza legs. They're extra criminal flavored! They're like goodness when your mom calls. And it's def time to call in my options. Hmmm—I could run away some more—except Ms. Pink Bloodhound here would no doubt track me down. I could try and kill this daft kraken—yeah, that's worked real good so far. Nope—my only hope was to go along, get along, give up, and give in. I am bitter with cunning! Most of which was sheer disgust—this cuttlefish wants nooky? Then nooky it shall get—maybe she'll slay me, maybe I'll cum, maybe we'll have babies, maybe I'll get bored—your usual spousal concerns. "You want hot beast sex?" I snarl. "Then big sex time it is." I even somehow conjure a boner up—hey, *you* try lusting after five tons of gooey fish pubes. "Alright! It's Miller time," Squidra yanks her tarp skirt off. "Um, no—baby," I wince, "please. Leave it on." Hey—no reason I gotta *look* at that puss. Or sniff it, ewww— Squidra must shower to help her social niche. But I kept my grit and spunk—at least the spunk—and got ready to do my part. Let's do our job with action! As I slide my kimono open, aim my swaying woody, shut my eyes, scream *geeraa* and run at her. Leave a shot of cheap rye and some towels on the sideboard, boys—if I survive I'm gonna need them. Survive? Hah—I'll be lucky to die in one piece. Give mom a kiss and dad a gat—put a candle in the window and a shiv up your butt—me, I'm going *in*.

25

Did we make lewd tangled love? Got me—I passed out within microseconds. Squid twats are *stanky*. Till much later I sat up like a drunk rocket. Was I dead yet? Happy stupid hoping! Nope—just choking on undersea slime. Which I spit out and glanced around for escape routes—that damned kraken would rear her fugly butt any second and demand more nooky. You know the rule—you bone it, you own it. But instead I bumped into a much naked chick. And not just any nude girl—this one was a stark fetal pink. She glowed like God's tongue. "You *do* love me," she traced a hand down my biceps, "but why you got such weak arms?"

"You should talk," I laughed, "you only got one." 'Cause her other arm was lopped off neat at the shoulder.

"No—I've got eight. Or is it ten? It *was* eight. God dammit—those silly gangstas must've chopped one off," she pointed at dead Yakuza. Actually everyone in here—bartenders, beer gnomes, sake hoes, and sloshed pilots—was killed except us. "Grrr, grrr," she growled, "they cut off my tentacle!"

"Your which what?" I was mondo confused—I need more brain for big knowing!

"My *tentacle*, dumb butt!" she screeched, ow.

"Uuuuurt?" I cocked my head like a cartoon dog.

"You *still* don't get it," that pink lass sulked, "I'm *her*."

"Her who?" I wiped gangsta goo off my ankle.

"I'm *Squidra*," she punched my shoulder, ow.

"Nah—I don't think so," I scoped her up and down, "can't be. Really?" Whoever she was, she was hotter than fried gold.

"Your kiss *changed* me," she licked her lips even pinker.

"Yeah," I shrugged, "I do have this spiritual effect on chicks, and—"

"No, dufus," she punched me harder, ow ow, "you changed me into a *human*."

"Um, I'm not sure how that works—" and why *did* she morph, anyway? Was it my smoochy human-growth hormone spunk what changed her? Was it fairies with goofer dust and Grimm pedigrees? Who cares—make something up. "And look here," that girl slapped her chest, "I got happy tits!"

"They *are* happy," I admired them. But even more than their upward lilt—more than their handy size and fragrant weight—they were this garish, DayGlo delirium-tremens baby elephant pink like the rest of her. She was a candy gestalt mixed from sleep and peach nougat with black fuzz sprinkles on her yummy puss. "Let's have more nooky," she cooed—and yep—she was def Squidra. My big ritual sex dick cured her—I am a hot weenie god! Pink girl, you're an unkempt vision—let's apply! Plus she still smelled like an unwashed ocean—that's how I knew she was her. "You seem surprised," Squidra giggled, grabbing my arm—ow—way too hard. "Oops," she grinned that trick smile, "I'm still way stronger than you, blue mansu." It was her smile what clinched it—you only see grins like that on drowned babies and anthropomorphic squids—that primordial smirk, the smile that splits the world alive. It's how wolves sneer when they smell gored ponies. It's how lightning beams when it spots a lone golfer. "Maybe we should get out of here," Squidra giggled, "want me to carry you?"

"With one arm? Good luck," I scowled. Hey, at least she ain't taller than me—or that dead pilot whose bloody raincoat I draped around her luscious bod. "Clothing?" she laughed, "why?"

"You'll get cold," I lied—actually she'd get us both arrested. It's one thing to smoosh Tokyo and even worse, a Yakuza bar—but even glittering pink ex-squid chicks can't walk around naked. Not when hordes of cops were hustling here—along with fireman and paparazzi and local sashimi maniacs greedy for a slice of trapped kraken. Like the wrapper on Drunky Cod brand entrails says—*Bring Mom these sushi guts*! "You're not making sense," human Squidra laughed.

"Never have," I shrugged.

"Excuse us—police," some cop knocked on a wall. You gotta love Japan—cops that knock! Anywhere else we'd be coroner meat already—here they still follow bizarre feudal norms. "Now where?" I checked around for exits—but they're all blocked! "Hmmm," I rummaged through splayed Yakuza bods, "maybe

we'd better find some hot guns and shoot the fuzz
when they—"

"Wait a sec," Squidra—or Girl-ra or whoever she
was now—blinked way too much. "I bet these still
work," and her eyes thrummed all ghastly Tang
orange till—whoa! Her eyeball lasers kicked in! And
toasted a skewed freezer to tin dust till a charred
doorway showed. "You still got *lasers*?" I gawked.

"Guess so," Squidra blinked her eyebeams off,
"doesn't everyone?"

"Probably," I fibbed. Look, I hadn't totaled the
math yet on our mutual power relations—and sure,
she's minus an arm—but eyeball lasers could def tip
the balance in her feminazi favor. Hello Gelding!
"Let's ditch this sake stand," Squidra buckled her
trench coat. "Lead on," I nodded as we snuck out a
back alley, our limbs and minds striding into night—
and that's it! That's enough—plots are more boring
than dead lawns. Let's snuff this sick puppy—join us
in book-shutting fun!

ABOUT RON DAKRON

Ron Dakron is the author of the novels *Hello Devilfish!*, *infra*, *Newt*, *Hammers*, and *Mantids*. His work runs the gamut from surrealism to sci-fi pastiche, with a prose style that he describes as "haplessly Chicagoan and influenced by working class whites, African American slang, and Yiddish comedy." His novels explore differing styles of poetic prose, from Romaticism to cubism, B-movie satire to mangled Japanese translation. Born in Chicago, Dakron majored in English at Elmhurst College and Lawrence University before moving to Seattle where he worked as a street violinist and house painter, and developed a con- frontational poetic performance style "drenched in faux punkery." He began writing novels in his late twenties, and considers himself "a proud working-class novelist who dreams up Big Lit." He lives in Seattle, WA.

Recent and Forthcoming Books from Three Rooms Press

PHOTOGRAPHY-MEMOIR

Mike Watt
On & Off Bass

FICTION

Ron Dakron
Hello Devilfish!

Michael T. Fournier
Hidden Wheel
Swing State

Janet Hamill
Tales from the Eternal Café
(Introduction by Patti Smith)

Eamon Loingsigh
Light of the Diddicoy

Richard Vetere
The Writers Afterlife

DADA

Maintenant:
Journal of Contemporary
Dada Art & Literature
(Annual poetry/art journal,
since 2008)

MEMOIR & BIOGRAPHY

Nassrine Azimi and
Michel Wasserman
Last Boat to Yokohama:
The Life and Legacy of
Beate Sirota Gordon

Richard Katrovas
Raising Girls in Bohemia:
Meditations of an American
Father; A Memoir in Essays

Stephen Spotte
My Watery Self:
An Aquatic Memoir

SHORT STORY ANTHOLOGY

Have a NYC:
New York Short Stories
Annual Short Fiction Anthology

PLAYS

Madeline Artenberg &
Karen Hildebrand
The Old In-and-Out

Peter Carlaftes
Triumph For Rent (3 Plays)
Teatrophy (3 More Plays)

MIXED MEDIA

John S. Paul
Sign Language:
A Painters Notebook

TRANSLATIONS

Thomas Bernhard
On Earth and in Hell
(poems by the author
in German with English
translations by Peter Waugh)

Patrizia Gattaceca
Isula d'Anima / Soul Island
(poems by the author
in Corsican with English
translations)

César Vallejo | Gerard Malanga
Malanga Chasing Vallejo
(selected poems of César Vallejo
with English translations and ad-
ditional notes by Gerard Malanga)

George Wallace
EOS: Abductor of Men
(poems by the author in English
with Greek translations)

HUMOR

Peter Carlaftes
A Year on Facebook

POETRY COLLECTIONS

Hala Alyan
Atrium

Peter Carlaftes
DrunkYard Dog
I Fold with the Hand I Was Dealt

Thomas Fucaloro
It Starts from the Belly and Blooms
Inheriting Craziness is Like
a Soft Halo of Light

Kat Georges
Our Lady of the Hunger

Robert Gibbons
Close to the Tree

Israel Horovitz
Heaven and Other Poems

David Lawton
Sharp Blue Stream

Jane LeCroy
Signature Play

Philip Meersman
This is Belgian Chocolate

Jane Ormerod
Recreational Vehicles on Fire
Welcome to the Museum of Cattle

Lisa Panepinto
On This Borrowed Bike

George Wallace
Poppin' Johnny

Three Rooms Press | New York, NY | Current Catalog: www.threeroomspress.com
Three Rooms Press books are distributed by PGW/Perseus: www.pgw.com